Secret Agent Sheikh

LINDA CONRAD

First published in Great Britain 2011
by Mills & Boon, an imprint of Harlequin (UK) Limited,
Large Print edition 2011
Eton House, 18-24 Paradise Road,
Richmond, Surrey TW9 1SR

© Linda Lucas Sankpill 2010

ISBN: 978 0 263 22347 7

Harlequin (UK) policy is to use papers that are natural,
renewable and recyclable products and made from
wood grown in sustainable forests. The logging
and manufacturing process conform to the legal
environmental regulations of the country of origin.

Printed and bound in Great Britain
by CPI Antony Rowe, Chippenham, Wiltshire

When asked about her favorite things, **Linda Conrad** lists a longtime love affair with her husband, her sweetheart of a dog named KiKi and a sunny afternoon with nothing to do but read a good book. Inspired by generations of storytellers in her family and pleased to have many happy readers' comments, Linda continues creating her own sensuous and suspenseful stories about compelling characters finding love.

A bestselling author of more than twenty-five books, Linda has received numerous industry awards, among them the National Reader's Choice Award, the Maggie, the Write Touch Readers' Award and the *RT Book Reviews* Reviewers' Choice Award. To contact Linda, read more about her books or to sign up for her newsletter and/or contests, go to her website at www.LindaConrad.com.

To Shelley and Peggy,
the most ingenious website
and newsletter creators ever!
You two are the greatest!

Chapter 1

Swinging in midair under an endless star-filled sky like some kind of superhero, Tarik Kadir held his breath until his feet reached the solid surface of the ledge.

Monte Carlo's tourists went about their business at sea level twelve stories below—oblivious to the drama unfolding high above their heads. Steadying himself, Tarik released the thin metal rappelling cable attached to the safety harness under his specially outfitted tuxedo shirt.

He let the line go loose and flattened his body against the stucco wall, stopping to let his pounding heart calm. But his heart continued thundering in his chest. Dropping over a dark abyss with nothing but air between your very existence and certain death was not his idea of smart.

The best part of his job had always been hiding in plain sight. Preferably at the nearest casino table. Becoming a different personality and handing people bold-faced lies was much more in keeping with his lifestyle than any crazy high-flying acrobatics needed to reach hotel ledges. After all, his brothers had always maintained that as the baby of the family, he'd excelled from earliest childhood at being a chameleon and making up stories.

He was born for his old job as a covert agent. But the Kadir family had recently asked all their sons to assume the responsibility for their growing war with ancient enemies, the Taj

Zabbar. Out of loyalty, Tarik resigned his commission with the United States Army immediately upon learning of his family's need for him to lead their intel-gathering efforts.

His foot slipped on the slick ledge and Tarik lost his balance. Grabbing hold of the uneven brick wall with his fingertips, he tried balancing on tiptoes. Looking out at the black expanse of ocean in the distance and the ant people strolling the seawall directly below, he swallowed back his panic and relied on innate athleticism to regain his balance.

Breathing slowly in and out, he made his way along the twelfth story ledge of Monte Carlo's Le Meridien Beach Plaza hotel. His thoughts turned to his former work as a member of a special para-military task force—a cross-branch compilation of Army Special Forces, Navy Seals and CIA spooks. He regretted having to quit and he missed working with some of the most elite men and women in the world of covert intelligence. His old unit had been special, known within the Department of Defense for its ability to track down international mobsters and terrorists while staying in the shadows.

With his heartbeat stabilized again, Tarik cleared his head, inching along in the darkness. As he reached the balcony of the penthouse suite, he slipped over the open railing and the half glass-wall enclosure and crouched down to conceal himself behind a potted palm. The balcony doors had been closed against the chilly night air, but he'd paid the maid a small fortune to see that the sliding glass was left unlocked for the night.

A secret power-broker meeting was supposedly about to take place in the suite on the other side of these glass doors. He needed to be in position with his high-tech surveillance and listening equipment before any of the action began.

Tarik peered past the edge of the glass. The room was an enormous space, set up with a temporary conference table surrounded by six captain's chairs. A handful of men had already gathered and were standing at a bar with drinks in their hands.

He recognized the Russian gangster who'd reputedly organized this little get-together from his CIA dossier. The gangster was Karolek Petrov, a renowned physics genius before the fall of the Soviet Union who had since amassed a $300 million empire based on illegal banking ventures and arms deals.

Tarik had to hand it to his older brother, Darin. His intel about this meeting had been spot-on.

As Tarik quietly set up the micro recording/ receiving device Darin's geek department had come up with, he rifled through his memory trying to put names to a couple of the other faces he'd recognized around the bar. Clearly none of the men were members of the Taj Zabbar. He and his brothers had turned themselves into experts at facial recognition when it came to their family's enemies. At this point he could pick out a Taj Zabbar face from any crowd.

Apparently not everyone had arrived for the meeting yet. The Taj Zabbar participant was the only one Tarik cared about, and he'd better show up soon.

Darin's technicians had gathered secret intelligence about this private auction a few days ago. It had been one of many dirty dealings the Kadirs had been anticipating from their enemies. The Taj Zabbar were going back into the international black market to buy arms. According to Darin's sources, the arms for sale at tonight's auction would be more along the lines of weapons of mass destruction.

Judging by Petrov's background, the

evening's prize would involve advanced technology. Either biological or nuclear.

Adjusting his earpiece, Tarik finished setting up and settled in to wait for the meeting to start. Crouching in the dark, he listened for anything important.

Tarik thought of Shakir, his middle brother, and of how he had recently destroyed an underground nuclear reactor plant in Zabbarán that had been designed by the Russians for the Taj Zabbar. The Kadir brothers had figured then it was only a matter of time before the Taj Zabbar tried to buy the nuclear capability they needed in the open market.

When the Kadirs had learned of tonight's private auction, Tarik had gone to his old boss at the Department of Defense, trying to enlist the Americans' help in gathering intel about the Taj Zabbar. Buying nuclear technology seemed a clear threat against the entire world rather than simple revenge against old enemies. But the DOD had been reluctant to commit, saying their resources were thin at the moment.

"Get me something tangible I can use to convince my superiors that this new third world nation of the Taj Zabbar is anywhere close to obtaining nuclear capabilities," General Wainwright had told him.

Tarik had tried to explain about the auction and had asked for help from his old unit in putting together a sting. Instead, when the general had turned him down flat, it had been a hard lesson in the futility inherent in a major bureaucracy.

One of the men in the room moved to the glass next to Tarik's head and stared out toward the moonlit sea. Tarik held his breath and eased farther back in the shadows, quickly coming up with a name for the face. The man was one of the Nigerian terrorists his old unit had recently been trying to locate. Here in Monte Carlo and about to bid on weapons of mass destruction?

Wouldn't the DOD love to know about the Nigerian's participation.

Tarik checked his equipment and made sure the video was being transmitted back to Darin's computers. This Nigerian terrorist alone would have been worth his old boss's attention.

As Tarik sensed the auction was about to start, a rap came at the suite's door. A heavyset man who looked a lot like the movie version of a Russian bodyguard went to answer.

Tarik's pulse rate picked up again. This had to be the Taj Zabbar representative at last.

Instead of a Taj Zabbar agent, a thin man sporting a mustache and wearing a gray tuxedo waltzed into the room with three beautiful women on his arm. Tarik was stunned. Expensive call girls at a secret auction like this?

His gaze flicked to the Russian, whose expression had gone cold. But the man did not make a move to expel the newcomers. Instead he offered them all drinks. It was odd behavior.

Tarik studied the new arrivals a little further. Something was not right.

One of the women laughed at the Russian's greeting, the sound of her voice reverberating deep and erotic in her throat. Something about that laugh…

He narrowed his eyes and looked closer, but she didn't look familiar. Her blond, pixie-cut hair was thick and shiny. Too shiny to be real. Her eyes were a violet color not often found in nature. Obviously the lady was trying to disguise herself and not doing it very well. But then, Tarik supposed, if he were a high-priced call girl, he might want to change his identity for each job, too.

He let his gaze rake down over her tight, compact body and the too-exposed expanses of exotic, tanned skin and felt a surprising thrill of recognition. Those curves had appeared in his dreams often enough.

What the hell…?

Another knock on the suite's door grabbed everyone's attention. When the new man and his entourage entered, Tarik sucked in a breath. Not only had the Taj Zabbar sent a representative to the auction, this one was none other than the Elder Nabil bin Khali Taj Zabbar—the general in charge of Taj Zabbar armed forces. With him was a bodyguard and another man Tarik believed to be the new head of Taj Zabbar secret police, Malik Kasim Taj Zabbar. The Taj Zabbar had sent their big guns.

CIA covert agent Jasmine O'Reilly worked hard not to fidget in her too-tight, scratchy dress while she surreptitiously checked out the men in the room as they greeted the newcomers. Who knew rhinestones could be this uncomfortable?

She was accustomed to wearing six-inch stilettos on special missions, but the flashy hooker-style dress was turning into more than she'd bargained for. How did women wear all these spangles and zippers? The simple answer came to her before she finished the question. The dress was not meant to be worn for long.

Pulling her attention back to the targets, she catalogued what she knew of them. The most important man in the room to her was not the Russian mafia character and his cohorts who'd called this meeting. No, with great glee she fixed her thoughts on the Nigerian terrorist she'd been after for the past six months.

God, was she ever good at her job.

Who else could've finagled their way into a room full of third world terrorists and wannabe bad guys? Certainly not that handsome but insufferable ex-agent, Tarik Kadir. She proudly noted that Kadir was nowhere to be found— even after he'd called the DOD's attention to this meeting in the first place.

Whatever was really going down here, Jass was about to make the premier bust of her entire career. She almost rubbed her hands together in satisfaction. But first she wanted to know about the rest of the players in addition to the Nigerian.

There was Karolek Petrov, of course. And a number of bodyguards. Then the high-priced pimp she'd paid to bring her and the other two phony call girls tonight. And if she wasn't mistaken, the other bidders included an Indonesian member of *al-Qaeda,* a rogue member of the IRA, a Georgian separatist and—hmm... The two Middle Eastern–looking newcomers were men who'd not been on her radar before. Interesting.

She supposed it was possible these were the repre-sentatives from the Taj Zabbar that Kadir had insisted were coming to buy tonight. But no one in her unit or their superiors had imagined he could be right.

Okay, the people known as the Taj Zabbar, from the new Republic of Zabbarán, had recently struck it rich with oil. Rich enough to buy whatever they wanted. But no rumors of their having terrorist leanings had reached the ears of the international intelligence communities. Why would the Taj Zabbar suddenly want to buy nuclear arms? Certainly not to attack the Kadir family as Kadir had insisted when he'd asked for assistance from the unit.

Perhaps it would be worth her effort to question Tarik Kadir at some point. However, tonight she was all about taking down the Nigerian. She wouldn't allow any of the other people in this room to stand in her way. She'd been after him and his information for six months.

Jass clicked her hidden mouthpiece twice to notify her backup that she was all set. According to the plan, two agents would burst through the door five minutes from her signal. That should be about right. By then everyone would be seated around the table and she could position herself close behind the Nigerian.

The Russian murmured to a bodyguard and a silver briefcase appeared on the table. Petrov nodded toward it and most of the men sauntered to their seats. All but the Middle Eastern men.

"Why are females in attendance?" the older one asked the Russian with a sneer.

"A prize for the losers tonight, Elder bin Khali." Karolek Petrov beamed as though he had a secret he couldn't wait to tell. "These are no ordinary women. Each represents a dozen young virgins who will give a man the night of his life before they gladly lay down their lives and die for him. They are worth a king's ransom…and are my gift for participating this evening."

Jass was glad the two actresses she'd rounded up looked young and didn't speak English. She tried to move farther away from the man Petrov had addressed as *Elder.*

But before she could take a second step, the younger Middle Eastern man grabbed her by the wrist. "This one is no virgin. If I am not mistaken, she is no lady of the evening either." He swung her around to face the other men. "Look at the intelligence in these eyes. She sees too much."

Jass didn't have a moment to react before the man brought a dagger to her throat. "I will let her fulfill her contract and die for my pleasure right now."

Oh, brother. There went all her best-laid plans.

She gritted her teeth to notify her backup with three clicks that she was in trouble. Then she overpowered her surprised assailant by using a nifty thumb hold she'd perfected years ago. The knife went flying and he went to his knees with a yell and a thud.

Chaos erupted in the room. Shouts in several languages bounced off the walls. Guns were pulled from under jackets. The door banged open and a shot rang out. And somewhere in the back of her mind she thought she heard the balcony's glass doors sliding open.

But she was too busy to notice. She appropriated a gun from one of the hulking bodyguards with a smooth move he never saw coming and then headed through the crowd toward the Nigerian, who had been standing closest to the balcony. She caught a glimpse of him before he ducked out through the open balcony doors.

Oh, no you don't. We're twelve stories up. You're mine, you bastard.

Tarik was inside the room and fighting to reach Jass O'Reilly before he could think twice about it. His mind had blanked when the head of Taj Zabbar secret police had put that dagger to her throat. Tarik had been intrigued with her from afar for years and the idea of his fantasy woman going down in a slash of bloodshed had moved him to action.

But by the time he overpowered the Russian and put him out of commission, she was nowhere to be found. Had she ducked out the front? Impossible. That exit was now clogged with men in various stages of being apprehended.

He twisted around and as his eyes darted across the room, he realized two unsettling things. The suitcase was missing from the table and the two Taj Zabbar reps were gone.

Worse, with another sweeping glance, he noted both the Nigerian and Jass had also disappeared. But they could not possibly have gotten past him. They'd both been too close to the balcony when the sting went bad.

He would have to consider the Taj Zabbar later. Right now he needed to back up his former comrade in covert operations.

When he barged through to the balcony, Tarik was hit with another shock. Jass and the Nigerian were leaning over the balcony wall, wrestling over a Ruger .357 Magnum. The Nigerian had a good fifty pounds and six inches on her.

Tarik's weapon was useless under the circumstances. He couldn't get off a clean shot. He held his breath and moved in closer, waiting for a moment to let the Nigerian learn of his presence—the hard way.

But the longer their struggle went on, the more he could see Jass weakening. The Nigerian had her bent over backward with her upper body hanging out over nothing but night air.

Tarik couldn't wait. He had to make a move now.

Grabbing the assailant by the shoulder, he tried to turn the Nigerian around to face him. But right at that moment Jass made her move, too.

She hooked her leg around the Nigerian's knees and used all her power trying to bring him down. But Tarik's shove had overbalanced the assailant and all three of them slid closer to the balcony wall.

Horrified, he watched as both Jass and the Nigerian slipped over backward and disappeared completely into the black night. With a roar, he dove over the wall, landing tenuously on the ledge beyond.

"Help me, you idiot." The small voice coming from below him finally cleared away the hazy panic in his head as Tarik spotted her fingers gripping the edge.

"Jass." He flattened himself on the ledge and made a grab for her arms.

When he felt the warm skin of her wrists and fastened his hands around them, he began to murmur quiet encouragement. "I've got you. Take it easy."

She groaned. "Stop talking and pull me up."

Earlier the breeze off the ocean had been benign and gentle. Now it felt like a full-force gale. He latched one arm around the balcony wall and hoped to hell he could drag her up one-handed. It would do no good for both of them to take a header into oblivion.

Whenever he'd thought of Jass in the past, he'd never thought of her as particularly thin or small. But with a spurt of much needed adrenaline, he raised her up over the edge without a lot of effort.

Son of a gun. They were still alive.

Dragging her closer to his chest, he waited until his breathing slowed and he could actually feel his extremities again. That was as close to death as he ever wanted to go.

Jass pushed at his chest. "How about we move to a solid surface?" She came to her knees and reached for the balcony wall. "I suppose you expect a thank-you for saving my life."

Suddenly irritated, he pulled them both over the wall to the balcony floor. "I would rather get an explanation as to why you felt it necessary to bust in on my sting."

She stood in bare feet with her wig askew and dusted off her hands. "Not your sting, pal. Mine. I've been chasing that Nigerian for months and now you've ruined our chances of ever questioning him. You owe me."

Damn.

"My mistake," he muttered as he turned toward the suite doors.

He left her standing there trying to figure out what he'd meant. If he'd known how ungrateful she would be, he might've left her swinging in midair.

Now he had the sinking feeling he was going to live to regret tonight's entire heroic episode.

Chapter 2

She was completely screwed.

Jass ran her hands through the auburn mop on her head that laughably passed for her real hair and squared her shoulders to face the music. Ed Langdon, her CIA handler, and General Gus Wainwright, the head of their interagency Task Force, came through the conference room door. Tarik Kadir was right on their heels.

She jumped up and stood as still as if she were at attention. It was barely twelve hours since the Nigerian had gone to his heavenly paradise and Jass hadn't had much sleep. For most of the night she'd been too busy trying to interrogate the men who'd been captured in the hotel room and, when that became futile, working desperately to salvage something from the fiasco of last night. She had come up empty-handed on all counts.

For the last hour she'd been sitting quietly in the American consulate's office waiting for her scheduled meeting with Ed. Jass had been going over all her moves from last evening's sting, still trying to piece together how things had gone wrong. When she'd originally designed the plan for last night, she was positive nothing could prevent it from becoming one of her biggest career highlights. Capturing a man that the Agency had been seeking for the last three years had seemed the perfect path to advancement.

The fact that General Wainwright was here in Monaco—that he'd felt it necessary to fly in from the states, did not bode well for her rising career at all. The general motioned for her to sit and she took her first breath since he'd walked through the door. Somehow she had to survive whatever came next with her job intact.

Tarik Kadir plopped down in the seat next to hers. Her senses started reeling. She could actually feel heat emanating from his body, even considering his place at the table was well over two feet away. She scooted her chair a little farther to the side, but it didn't help.

Glancing at the ex covert agent out of the corner of her eye, she found him staring back at her. Besides being insufferable, the man was also a rude bore.

He flashed her a crooked grin from behind his benign-looking black-framed glasses. Was he in some sort of disguise this morning? She knew for a fact that the man did not need glasses for his eyesight. Last night in a tux he'd been delicious to look at. Like the billionaire playboy sheik he was rumored to be. But this morning, the hand-tailored button-down shirt and soft suede jacket made him look unpretentious and conservative.

Bull. Did he really believe anybody would miss the aura of controlled power or the watchful intelligence hiding underneath the traditional cut of his coal-colored hair or in the eyes behind those ridiculous fake glasses?

"You still waiting for a thank-you for saving my life?" she asked while trying hard to sound unaffected.

"I don't waste much time on fantasies." The look he gave her was so full of erotic meaning it sent her pulse racing and made her mouth go dry.

She tried to inch farther away but found herself hugging the wall as Ed and General Wainwright seated themselves across the table.

The general's forehead furrowed as he began, "Well, Special Officer O'Reilly. It seems your crack plan for capturing the Nigerian turned into a royal cluster f..." He stopped, looked slightly flustered about almost using the crude military expression meaning disaster, and then cleared his throat. "Either of you two have anything more to say about what happened last night?"

"Everything would've worked out if *he* hadn't stepped in."

"If the DOD had listened to me about the Taj Zabbar building weapons of mass destruction in the first place, *we* could've worked this sting together and nothing would've been lost."

They'd both spoken at the same time and their words were more or less blown away in the confusion. Exasperated, Jass folded her arms over her chest and sat back.

The general pinned her with a steely gaze. "Did it once occur to you to ask what item could've been big enough to induce the

Nigerian to come out of the shadows and attend last night's sale?"

"I figured it was big drug deal or maybe U.S. counterfeit currency plates, sir. Rumor has it the Nigerian has been raising funds and buying into moneymaking schemes all over Europe." Jass was becoming more uncomfortable by the second.

The general waved his hand dismissively. "My fault. I should've seen this coming when I approved your plan."

Next he turned on Tarik. "You thought you recognized Special Officer O'Reilly in her disguise. Is that right?"

Tarik nodded once.

"And yet you went out on the balcony to rescue someone you knew to be a competent officer and turned your back on the briefcase containing a nuclear device."

Tarik's face paled and his jaw became impossibly hard.

The general surprised him by flashing a grin. "I guess we're all treading in deep water over this screwup. Let's see what we can do to make it right."

Jass didn't like the sound of that. She had no intention of ever doing anything with the infuriating *sheik* Kadir.

Tarik could see the frustration building on Jass's face. He knew what that was like. He'd been trying for months to convince the DOD, and General Wainwright in particular, that the Taj Zabbar were a serious and growing danger to the world. Up until this morning, he hadn't succeeded.

He forced his attention back to the general. "I just finished speaking to my brother at Kadir headquarters, sir. The briefcase has disappeared—along with the Elder bin Khali Taj Zabbar. We'll pick him up again, though it might take some time. But Darin did get a line on that other matter you asked about." He took a breath. "Seems our technical unit has been hearing the same rumors over the social networks that your units have, and we're fairly sure the Taj Zabbar will be involved in that upcoming auction, too."

"Then that gives us a place to start fresh together." The general tilted his head to address Jass. "We caught a break when another DOD split task force captured an *al-Qaeda* operative in Pakistan last week. The Pakistanis have been interrogating the man and yesterday obtained a major piece of intel."

Tarik watched as Jass's expression went from resigned and frustrated to hopeful and eager. She was arresting to look at with her exotic mix of cultures. Not classically beautiful, but expressive and fascinatingly intense when she thought she wasn't being observed. A man couldn't avoid keeping his eyes trained on that face. At least, not this man.

"It seems our Russian from last night's auction had another partner," the general continued. "Someone still operating in the wind who supposedly has one more auction scheduled for next week."

"Another briefcase bomb? Surely not. That's—"

The general's hand chopped the air to stop her words. "No, another bomb would've been impossible to sneak out of Russia, even for a genius like Karolek Petrov. But it seems there is one more item up for bid that's worth paying a king's ransom—at least for terrorists."

Jass sat up a little straighter. "A detonator or timing device of some sort?"

"Good point. It's possible. We don't know for sure." General Wainwright folded his hands on the desk and stared down at them. "Whatever it is, it's big. All we know are the identities of some of the bidders and the approximate location and date. We need to know the rest."

Jass's eyes rounded and dilated. Bless her fiendish little heart. Tarik could see she was almost drooling over the potential of being given such a plum assignment. When she learned the truth, that this was going to be his sting—not hers—he had a feeling her expressive face would be speaking a different language.

"Do we have a way to firm up the location?" Jass asked the general.

She was starting to believe this would be more of a golden opportunity rather than the end of her career. She snuck a look at Ed, her handler, and was puzzled by his narrowed expression. He apparently knew something she did not.

"The auction will definitely be taking place in Brazil," the general answered with authority. "The Russian's partner, also one of the Russian mob but not as clever as Petrov, has developed a network headquartered in Rio. That much we know for sure. The Kadir family's intel unit has put feelers out and we expect to have better information as we get closer to the date."

The *Kadir family* intel unit? What the heck was that? And what the devil was wrong with their own CIA intelligence? No wonder Ed was not looking too happy.

Jass pinned her lips together to keep from making a remark she might regret later. She was still convinced she was only a hairsbreadth away from being kicked out of the Task Force over last night's screwup. The way this new mission turned out would make all the difference to her career.

She had to keep her job. It was her only chance to live up to the high standard her father set years ago. Thank God it appeared she was being given the opportunity.

"Special Officer O'Reilly, your background file says you can speak both Russian and Farsi.

Is that correct?" The general had his gaze trained on her face.

"Yes, sir. My mother's family was originally from Iran and I spoke Farsi before English. I learned the Russian language for a covert op a few years back."

"Well, Farsi is not perfectly suited for this mission but we can make it work. The Russian is pivotal."

He was going to make her the operative in charge of the mission after all! Relief nearly brought her to tears. Jass was thrilled to get the badly needed superior position to make up for the one she'd messed up. Taking a deep breath, she turned to study Kadir. What was his role here? Informant? Adviser?

Whatever it was, she hoped they wouldn't have to work together too closely or for terribly long. The man rode her nerves whenever his gaze raked over her body. Which was pretty much every time she'd ever run into him.

"We've devised a sting to take advantage of a couple of lucky breaks." The general turned to Ed for an affirmative nod, then continued. "First, about a month ago, ICE agents apprehended a woman who's been on Homeland's watch list for years. She's an international illegal arms dealer with no allegiance to any country and who seems devoid of any scruples about the deals she makes."

"The *Messenger?*" Jass knew of only one woman who might fit that criteria.

The general nodded grimly. "As a favor to us, Homeland has kept the lid on her capture. We're sure nothing has leaked out to any of the intelligence community."

Jass was positive he was correct. She'd been following the exploits of the mysterious woman known as the Messenger for years and knew nothing of her capture.

Turning to Tarik, the general explained further. "This shadowy female dealer's real name is Celile Kocak. Originally Uzbekistani from Russian and Turkish decent, as I understand. Her exploits in the field of buying and selling arms have been embellished over time, yet no one had ever seen a picture of the woman.

"Now that we have her in custody," he went on. "It turns out she has a few years on Special Officer O'Reilly. But other than that, the two could easily pass as sisters."

Wow. Think of that. The mysterious woman who had captured her imagination for forever looked enough like her to be a sister. Jass was enthralled by the idea of passing for such a deadly and merciless criminal on a sting.

From his position next to her, Tarik cleared his throat. "You said there'd been two lucky breaks?"

"Indeed. Under intense interrogation we've learned that this Kocak woman has been scouring the market for the last few months, looking for special arms to buy for another mysterious character. A shady Middle Eastern sheik who goes by the name of Abu Zohdi. We've been trying to track him down, and he's recently turned up in an English jail in the Bahamas—although they didn't know who they had in custody.

"This middle-easterner is one extremely dangerous and rich terrorist," the general went on to explain. "With close ties to *al-Qaeda*. And the Bahamians were about to release him due to lack of evidence. It was only by pure luck that we obtained his whereabouts from the Kocak woman before he was long gone."

"We have Abu Zohdi in our hands now?" Jass knew that name too and was beginning to worry about where the general's explanation was heading.

"Momentarily. In the meantime we are continuing to interrogate the Kocak woman, trying to learn what kind of arms will be for sale in Rio."

Yes, the more information she had before going in, the better prepared she would be to disrupt the sale. "Excuse me, General Wainwright, but what result do you anticipate from our mission? Is it more important to capture this other Russian or to take control of whatever weapons are for sale?"

The general raised one eyebrow and she almost giggled at the silly picture he made. "I trust you will not hesitate to confiscate anything as potentially dangerous as a nuclear bomb if it's placed right in front of you, Officer O'Reilly. Not this time."

Her smile faded in that instant. She felt her cheeks warming and was glad for her golden skin tones. Fairer women had a more difficult time disguising their embarrassment.

"Yes...uh...no, sir."

"Your job on this sting is to get your partner inside that auction to meet all the bidders. Gather information. Intel is your ultimate

assignment with the Task Force, remember."
The general narrowed his eyes at her. "Your
handler will give you further instructions once
we get a clearer picture of what's going on
inside."

"My partner?" Jass's whole body tensed.

"Kadir here will be going in undercover as
your client, Abu Zohdi. For months he's been
trying to convince the DOD that the Taj Zabbar
have become terrorists worthy of our attention." He spoke in a low, measured tone. "If
they do show up at this meeting ready to buy,
my boss will have to accept that they're powerful enough to pose a threat to the world."

Jass's mind raced with good reasons why she
couldn't take Tarik Kadir along with her on a
mission. The number-one reason being that he
was no longer employed by the United States
government. He'd quit.

Tarik stirred in his seat beside her. They shot

a glance at each other. He didn't seem all that thrilled about working with her either.

"But sir, I respectfully ask you to reconsider," she pleaded. "I can handle this mission better alone. If you want to know the identities of the people at the auction, leave it to me. I'll get names, pictures and backgrounds on everyone involved with no trouble. It's my *job*."

"Besides," she continued, desperately trying to come up with a good argument in her favor. "Doesn't the Messenger always work alone? On behalf of a client, for sure, but haven't her past clients always remained unnamed?"

"Not recently. Your intelligence on the Messenger is at least a year behind. You'd better study her files carefully on your way to Rio."

"But…"

The general tilted his head toward her as if to say he was done with her questions. But then he made one more chilling remark to top off his side of the argument and leave no doubt why this sting would go down exactly his way.

"Over the last year, Celile Kocak and Abu Zohdi have become lovers. According to her, they seldom leave each other's sides. In fact, that's how ICE got their hands on her. She made a mistake in her haste through the States to the Bahamas trying to reach her lover and bail him out of jail."

Lovers? Oh, Lord.

She felt Tarik go rigid in his seat beside her as he asked, "Lovers, sir? Exactly how close to that definition do you want us to stay?"

"Close enough for it to appear you can't keep your hands off each other, Mr. Kadir. This joint mission was originally your idea. And you agreed to accept one of our Task Force agents as your partner."

The general glared at both agents.

"Now stick to the plan we've drawn up. You two are going in as lovers or the whole deal is off."

Chapter 3

Jass's knees were still trembling an hour after her meeting with General Wainwright. She'd finally shed the scratchy dress for her jeans, but her mind continued racing with possible scenarios for escape.

She couldn't imagine having to work with the irritating sheik. Now, while sitting alone across from Ed having coffee, she had the feeling she'd stepped onto a boat that was taking on water.

"I don't like it any better than you do, Jass.

He's a loose cannon and I'm not sure we can trust him."

Ed Langdon, her longtime friend as well as her handler, ran a hand across tired-looking eyes. The poor guy hadn't had any more sleep than she had last night.

"But we don't have a choice." He sighed and stared into his coffee. "You have to at least go through the motions of this sting with Kadir or else Wainwright may bust us both out of the Task Force."

"Oh, Ed. No. Whatever I screwed up had nothing to do with you."

He dug his fingers through his thinning hair and then went back to drinking coffee with both hands wrapped around the mug. "You're my responsibility. When an assignment goes bad, it's my fault."

Ed was the closest thing to a father figure she'd had since her own father died on a CIA covert mission nearly ten years ago. At that time she had recently graduated college and was interviewing with the Agency for her first job. Her father had wanted her to go to law school. He'd wanted something safer and saner for his daughter than he'd had for himself.

But she'd always seen her father as the sun, the moon and the brightest star in the sky. Everything revolved around him and had since her mother died when she was a girl. What her father did for a living was exciting. Stimulating. The very idea of undercover work had thrilled her down to her bones.

Her mother had been the steady one in the family. The rock. She'd had a nice, normal job as an accountant. And what did that get her? She'd been kidnapped from her nice safe office, robbed and murdered.

No thanks. Jass would take her chances with undercover work.

"I don't like the whole idea of this Kadir character forcing himself on you while you try to make an ill-conceived plan work. He's charismatic when he wants to be."

Jass bristled. "Geez, Ed. You know me better than that. No one takes advantage of Jasmine O'Reilly."

Ed gave her a lopsided smile. "I know, honey. Sometimes I think you take yourself far too seriously. How long has it been since you've even had a date?"

"Uh, a while. I've been working. It's hard to go out when you're playing the part of a dangerous Indonesian spy or in disguise as the girlfriend of an IRA terrorist." She shrugged. "But I don't feel deprived. I like undercover work. A lot."

Ed grinned. "Yep. Too damned independent and serious for your own good. You can't go through your whole life like that, you know."

After her father had died, Ed had gone to bat for her at the Agency. He'd been her father's partner and longtime friend and said he wanted to help her however he could. And when Ed was promoted to being SAC and a handler, he'd made sure she was under his wing and came along, too. He'd always been every bit as concerned about her as a person as he was with her as a covert officer under his control.

Jass fiddled with her paper napkin. "I have lots of time for a life later. I'm only twenty-nine. You know how important it is to me to be the best at what I do."

Ed sat silent for a few moments. Finally he said, "Look, you have to take this assignment. But you don't have to fall for whatever Kadir is selling. I believe he has his own agenda and will try to gain your trust so he can somehow get his hands on the prize." He looked at her intently. "Don't let him. As usual, I'll be standing by to remind you to keep your head in the game. Listen to me."

"Don't I always?" she murmured, smiling at Ed.

He blew out a breath and chuckled. "Okay, little girl. Good enough for now. Let's see about getting you prepped for whatever surprises come your way."

Tarik had to force his gaping mouth shut when Jass climbed into the back of their limo with him. Man, did she look hot. Not that she didn't always look terrific, with her sexy auburn hair, exotic hazel-green eyes and a body to drool over.

But this sophisticated persona of the deadly Celile Kocak sent electric shivers straight to his groin. Maybe their mission wouldn't be hard to take after all.

The CIA handler, Ed, slammed the limo's back door after her and slid into the front seat next to the driver. "You all set, Kadir?"

Tarik wasn't paying much attention to Ed. He had better things to look at. Dressed in one of those French-designed suits and Italian leather four-inch heels, Jass never turned her head his way. She kept staring out the window as the limo began to roll away from the hotel.

Tarik absently adjusted his gold-braided head scarf and spoke to Ed without turning. "Becoming a rich Middle Eastern sheik is one disguise that shouldn't be too much of a problem for me, Langdon."

He kept his eyes trained on Jass. "You look amazing. Run into any trouble with the background intel?"

She turned her head only slightly and a strand of that long, luxurious mane slid over one dark-brown contact, obscuring it from his view. "I know how to do my job."

If it wasn't a balmy, late winter day in Monte Carlo, Tarik would've expected an ice storm. Much more of that kind of cold shoulder and this assignment might be the death of him yet.

"Well, I wish one of you could speak Portuguese," Langdon added from the front seat. "A dozen languages between you and yet not the one that might save your ass in Brazil."

"Spanish is close enough," Tarik said without as much as a smirk on his face. "We can fake it."

Jass shot him another icy, half-hidden glare and inched closer to her door. "You can bet the *Cariocas* will notice we don't speak their language."

"We're going in as tourists," he argued. "Arms buyers. Not Rio natives. We'll get along."

Tarik heaved a heavy sigh and leaned back in his seat. Yes indeed, this was going to be one long, miserable assignment. And if they couldn't find some middle ground, they'd both be lucky to come away from it alive.

A few hours later, flying high above the Atlantic, Tarik loosened the seat belt in his first-class seat and checked on Jass. He thought she might be trying to sleep, but she was wide awake and working on her laptop. She had the privacy screen set on the laptop so no one could read over her shoulder and she looked for all the world like any wealthy international businesswoman.

They needed to begin bonding. He'd let her put an aisle between them for the flight. But the minute they left the relatively secluded confines of this first-class cabin and moved into the duel worlds of espionage and glitz in Rio, they would have to begin the lovey-dovey act. The snow princess would have to thaw or the entire mission would be compromised.

He cleared his throat, moved into the empty seat beside her and pitched his voice low enough to be heard only by her. "I understand you keep an apartment in D.C. How long has it been since you've been home?"

She flipped down the laptop's lid and turned her head, pushing back the thick veil of hair covering the side of her face. "You've been reading my file? Maybe it would be better if you stuck to studying the files concerning Celile and Zohdi."

"We only have a few hours to work on becoming an intimate couple." How could she rile him this quickly? "I thought it would be smart for us to get to know each other a little better on a personal level first."

Jass frowned and drew a weary breath. "Fine. D.C. is not my home. I was raised in Chicago by my mother's family—which of course you know if you've read my file. But the apartment in D.C. is a few blocks from where my father used to keep his base while working for the Agency. As a kid I visited him between assignments and I know a little about the neighborhood. Still, it isn't what I would call a real home.

"When you come right down to it," she added quietly. "I don't guess I have what most people would call a home. Never felt the need for one."

Ah, but the wistful tone in her voice said that last statement was a lie. Tarik filed the interesting bit of information away for a later time when he'd gotten to know her better.

"But that's something we have in common," he murmured. "See? We haven't been talking for more than a few moments and already we've found a subject to agree on. None of the extended Kadir family have formal roots either. Not for a thousand years. We're…"

"Nomads," she supplied. "Originally Bedouins. Yes, I read your file, too."

He felt ridiculously pleased that she'd cared enough to read his file. Not that he should have doubted it. Whatever else Ms. Jasmine O'Reilly turned out to be underneath her many personas, she was a serious and dedicated CIA operative. She would never go on a mission unprepared, even one that had been as spur of the moment as this one.

The flight attendant brought them both

glasses of white wine. Jass took a sip before thanking the fellow and sending him away.

"Why did you resign your commission?" she asked as she studied Tarik over the rim of her glass. "The files weren't clear on that point."

Ah yes, the billion-dollar question. He knew the men in his old Special Forces unit and many of his former comrades in the joint Task Force were asking themselves the same thing. Well, he wanted to become closer to Jass for this mission. Might as well tell her all of it.

"I doubt my file has a notation in it explaining the five-hundred-year-old family feud between the Kadir family and the Taj Zabbar tribes of Zabbarán. It's something my brothers and I barely understand ourselves."

Jass set down her wine but kept her eyes trained on his face. "I discovered a little about the feud by doing a Google search. Originally, the Kadirs were caravan traders on the Spice Route. And around five hundred years ago the caravan was decimated by the fierce Taj Zabbar tribes. Right so far?"

He nodded, fascinated by her low, hypnotic voice.

"Yes, well. Apparently the Kadirs turned around and destroyed as many of the Taj Zabbar as they could in retaliation."

"Hold on. Our side of the story is a lot different. The Kadirs had no choice. We had to neutralize the threat in order to survive. The Taj wouldn't stop. They kept on coming. They…"

He stopped himself mid-rant and forced a smile when her eyes gleamed with humor. "Okay, I agree. That was centuries ago and no real written records were kept at the time. It could've happened the way you said. And at a much later date we weren't exactly angels when it came to our treatment of the Taj."

"Ah yes," she interrupted. "Let's jump the story ahead to fifty years ago when the Kadirs were already filthy rich in the shipping industry and looking to further their interests in the Zabbarán territory." She quirked a brow. "Didn't your family make a secret deal with the Taj Zabbar's neighbors and oppressors, the Kasht? Supposedly the Kadirs traded guns and other armaments for the sole rights to the only deep-water port in Zabbarán and the surrounding area. Right?

"Now that was really some Spice Trade." She'd added her own answer with a wry smile. "And didn't the Kasht use those very weapons to subdue a revolt by the Taj? They killed Taj women and children, put the men into slave labor and then burned and pillaged everything in sight. Nice family trade, Kadir." A note of derision filled her voice. "Why am I not even a little surprised that the Taj hate your family and want revenge?"

Tarik tamped down on the automatic rise in his blood pressure. He knew the truth of what his family had done and who they were now.

The Kadir family's past was not spotless. But in more modern times they had become contributing members of civilized world society—unlike their counterparts the Taj Zabbar.

"I don't have to defend my family to anyone. Everything you said may be true, but it was done long ago. Before either of us was born. And it's no excuse for the Taj to behave the way they do today." His eyes hardened. "They're terrorists, killers and brutes. They deal with drug lords and mobsters the world over. They've tried to annihilate my family by blowing us up, and never mind that fifty innocent people were caught in the explosion."

He took a breath and let the words roll out. "They kidnap vulnerable women and sell them to the highest bidders. They run their own country like a medieval fiefdom, even with all their new wealth. And worst of all, they are secretly planning to become the world's newest nuclear power before any of the civilized nations can take notice."

"How do you know that last part? About their nuclear ambitions."

She had genuine interest in her eyes for the first time since he'd begun speaking. The new expression made her look young...vulnerable, and made Tarik damned curious about getting to know this part of her a lot better.

"My middle brother Shakir went into Zabbarán covertly a few months ago to rescue the woman who has since become his wife. She and their son were being held for trade to the highest bidder," he explained. "I was part of my brother's backup team. While we were there, we found an underground nuclear centrifuge facility and..."

"What?" Jass leaned in close and pinned him with a doubtful look. "From what I understood the Taj are too backward and couldn't possibly have that kind of scientific know-how."

"Just listen," he began, instead of counting to ten to calm his temper. "I have in my possession a few satellite photos of the area under construction. And the images seem clear enough to people in the know. But we blew the place up before we left the country. I figured why not take the opportunity and save the rest of the world a hell of a lot of grief."

Jass leaned back in her seat. "So you don't have any real proof. Only wild speculation and fuzzy pictures."

He bristled but kept his voice down. "I was there. And our family's intelligence units have been picking up further mentions of nuclear subjects in the current Taj communiqués. We're sure they haven't given up their ambitions."

"How so?" she probed.

"Look at the other night. They sent a couple of representatives to that auction and stole the briefcase bomb, didn't they?"

"Did they? We only have your word on that.

I wouldn't know what they look like. The Taj aren't on the world intelligence radar screens." She smirked at him. "Those Middle Eastern men in the room that night could've just as easily been members of the Kadir clan for all I know."

Frustrated, Tarik sat back and stared out the window before he made a few remarks that would be totally inappropriate for anyone who intended to become her lover within the next few hours. He was usually much better at capturing a woman's attention and interest than this. In fact, he was *always* better at convincing people of his honesty and sincerity. Ironically, that was part of what made him such a good covert agent.

What was with Jass O'Reilly? He'd known she was slightly different than most women. But she wasn't even responding to him like a normal human being.

He was foundering here, trying to find some

common ground. What the hell would happen when they had to pretend to have an intimate love affair?

Jass was a pro. She didn't need Tarik Kadir to remind her of their mission. But he'd tried to do exactly that as they left the plane and entered Rio's Galeao Airport. She'd sniffed at his ridiculous attempt to rile her and brushed out past the flight attendants.

Throwing her tote bag over her shoulder, she sidled up close to him on their walk to retrieve the baggage and whispered low, "Don't forget Zohdi wouldn't let Celile carry anything heavy—or walk too far ahead. It's part of his macho personality."

Tarik's body jerked, almost imperceptibly, but he slowed enough to reach around and take her tote with a huge grin. "Here, let me, my darling." He used a clear, slightly accented voice.

"Wouldn't want to tire you before we reach the hotel. I have big plans for us later tonight."

She ground her teeth and smiled seductively. "Of course, sweetheart. But business comes first."

Fortunately for her, another part of Zohdi's personality was deeply rooted in his Middle Eastern background. He did not indulge in sentimental bodily contact in public. No pawing or slobbery kisses for him. She almost reminded Tarik of that, but decided to keep her mouth shut for now.

Zohdi never let his gaze stray from the love of his life for long. And he never let her talk to another man without putting himself close enough to feel her pulse beat.

Jass thought that last part might've been romantic if the two people in question weren't such a dangerous duo. And if her undercover partner on this romantic assignment wasn't Tarik Kadir.

The Rio airport terminal was a madhouse. Crowds descended from every corner and surrounded them as they walked. Jass felt the tension building in her every cell. While she was undercover, she never cared for crowds. An assassin could easily attack from any direction and she wouldn't recognize the threat until it was too late.

When they finally reached the baggage carousel, they found the crowds impenetrable around it. This much congestion in the Rio airport on a Thursday evening seemed strange—and she wondered if it could potentially signal a glitch in their mission.

The two of them stood motionless at the edge of the crowd for a moment as they silently pondered their best plan of attack for reaching the luggage.

"Ms. Kocak. Sheik Zohdi." Suddenly a man who seemed to be a native Brazilian spoke to them with a heavy accent. He'd appeared out of nowhere right beside them. "I am your driver. Your luggage is being sent ahead. Please follow me."

Jass raised her shoulders along with her gut instincts. Ed had told her they would be contacted by someone from the CIA station chief's office with further instructions. But she hadn't expected anyone this soon.

She glanced at Tarik, who also seemed to be on alert, but then he gave her a cockeyed grin and inclined his head. "After you, love. I am yours to command."

He was silently signaling that he was leaving the choice to follow this man up to her. Her whole body trembled with pride and an odd sensual awareness as she forced herself to turn and make her way through the throngs behind the stranger.

That grin of Tarik's might end up becoming her undoing before their assignment was over. The man was impossibly handsome all dressed up as a modern sheik in his Versace suit, white linen boat-necked shirt and head scarf. Jass shook off the sensual pull she'd felt and worked her mind back to the persona of Celile.

She had to remember that Ed said not to trust Tarik despite his glib manner and sincere looks.

They reached the curb in front of the airport and found a sleek black sedan waiting. Their driver paid two thugs who were obviously carrying concealed weapons and, with a few words in Portuguese, sent them on their way. Then he ushered her and Tarik into the backseat.

As they pulled into the stop-and-go traffic, she asked the driver, "What's going on here? Why all the people and congestion?"

Suddenly their driver didn't have even a slight accent. "You're kidding, right? Tomorrow is the start of *Carnivale*. The tourists are pouring into the city. Expect the crowds to get a lot worse over the next four days."

"Smart." Tarik relaxed back into his seat and

propped an ankle over his knee. "The Russian picked the best time of year to hold this little auction. His buyers will be tough for us to pick out from the rest of the tourists."

She turned to see Tarik in the dim light filtering in through the car's windows. "Have you ever been to Rio's *Carnivale* before?"

"Several times. You're going to love it. All sensual music, body heat and very little clothing." He chuckled under his breath. "It's guaranteed to warm up the chilliest woman on earth. Even the ice queen Celile Kocak doesn't stand a chance during *Carnivale*."

Oh hell. The man was doing his damnedest to unnerve her. Well, no matter what Tarik Kadir sent her way, she wouldn't let him throw her. She would remain in control.

After all, Jass O'Reilly was a pro.

Chapter 4

Tarik led the way through the grand lobby of the Copacabana Palace Hotel. The towering sixty-foot columns and ornate glass chandeliers were familiar, but the feeling of being watched was unique.

He liked crowds. Liked the anonymity of getting lost in the confusion. When their driver had first reminded him of *Carnivale,* Tarik's brain began processing new ways of completing their mission over the next few days. He'd thought of the festivities as a terrific idea for a cover.

But he hadn't counted on having the exotic and stunning faux Celile Kocak in tow. Every male head in the cavernous lobby turned to stare as she walked past. No wonder Sheik Zohdi seldom let more than a few feet pass between them in public.

Tarik tried to control the possessive urges he felt toward her. In reality the woman beside him was not the ice queen. Instead she was Jass O'Reilly, every bit as gorgeous as Celile but ten times more annoying. Everything he said seemed to strike her the wrong way. Despite his usual charm and glib small talk, she'd refused to warm up.

But that didn't mean his body didn't grow too warm every time he looked her way. Damned woman was hot. Both in the guise of Celile and out. And he figured she was going to make him sweat a lot more before this mission was over.

"We've already registered you two," their driver said quietly. "And your suite's checked and clean. We'll be able to go over mission specifics without being overheard."

So…while they'd been in the air, the Task Force had been busy devising a plan. Good enough. Tarik needed to keep his head in the game—and off his partner.

After they settled into the three-room suite and double-checked for listening devices and cameras, the driver nodded toward the dining table. "We couldn't secure a penthouse suite on such short notice at this time of year, but I hope you'll be comfortable here."

Jass removed her jacket and plopped into one of the chairs around the table. "It'll do for Celile and Zohdi. They're not on vacation."

"Well," their driver began as he set up the rest of the chairs around the table. "This is the honeymoon suite. Part of your cover story is that the two of you are taking a romantic interlude while you wait for the upcoming auction."

"Uh…" Jass jumped up, looking a little green

around the edges. "Excuse me a moment." She grabbed her jacket off the back of a chair and headed straight for the bedroom.

"Do we know yet when the auction is supposed to take place?" Tarik gladly reached for any excuse to put the spotlight back on the mission and take it off his errant libido.

The driver turned to him with his hand outstretched and not a trace of accent in his English. "We haven't met, Kadir. The name's João Bosque, CIA station chief. Have a seat."

Tarik joined him at the table. "What do we know?"

"Coincidentally, we've been keeping an eye on this Russian character you're after. His name is Andrei Eltsin. He blew into Rio several months ago and immediately took over the territory and operation of one of our *bicheiros*—those are the gang operators of this city's illegal lottery." Bosque scooted his chair closer.

"We inserted a man inside Eltsin's *bicheiro*

about a month ago. Their headquarters is in a penthouse above a nightclub in the Lapa district." Bosque poured himself a cup of the strong Brazilian coffee that had been placed on the table along with a basket of fresh fruit. "Our inside man is there gathering intel on their money-laundering operations. We're sure some of those billions are going to fund terrorism operators in the U.S."

Tarik nodded and sat back. "Okay. But what about the auction?"

"Our man isn't positive where, but he believes it's to be held on the last night of *Carnivale*. Fat Tuesday."

"Makes sense. But…"

"It's supposed to take place in Eltsin's retreat in the mountains right outside the city." Jass added the new info as she floated back into the room, looking light and airy in a floral silk pants outfit. "I received a message from Ed. He's on his way into the country, taking a military transport. Seems the real Celile was…convinced…to contact Eltsin and put her name on the bidders list for Tuesday. We're in."

"Fast work." Tarik couldn't keep from staring. His real-life partner, the covert agent, had become a real-live piece of art in cool shades of green and blue. And her movements were those of a lithe dancer as she crossed the room.

"The CIA has a convincing team of interrogators working with Celile and Zohdi." Jass picked up an apple and took a bite with relish.

Drooling at the sight, all Tarik could think at that moment was that he was glad his name wasn't Adam. This *Eve* was already tempting him enough to send him straight to hell.

The honeymoon suite. Jass's knees still wobbled at the idea, but she wouldn't give Kadir the satisfaction of seeing her sweat. They could straighten out the sleeping arrangements later—when she'd taken control of the mission again. In the meantime she would sleep on the couch or in the bathtub if necessary.

"Do we know what item we're supposed to bid on?" Tarik looked slightly annoyed.

What did he have to be annoyed about? He was on this mission despite her reservations. He should be grateful.

"No," she managed past another bite of apple. "Celile honestly doesn't know. And our interrogators couldn't devise a way for her to ask Eltsin without sounding suspicious either. We're going to need—"

"Reconnaissance," Tarik interrupted. "Our intel unit will continue gathering info from the underground."

And by *our intel unit* he meant the Kadir family? She opened her mouth to complain when Tarik stood and backed away from the table.

"Come on," he said as he took her hand and

pulled her to her feet beside him. "Put on your dancing shoes."

He drew her into his arms and pulled her close. Too close.

"How rusty are your samba skills, darling?" He'd whispered those words into her temple, but she could swear she felt the pounding of his heart right through both their clothes. "Need a few quick lessons?"

With the way he was holding her, that question could have a double meaning. She tried to pull away, but he held her fast.

"I'll match my samba skills to yours anytime, *darling*." She could barely believe how parched her voice sounded.

Tarik chuckled and released her. "We'll see about that. Now go put on your sexiest shoes—and take off most of your clothes. Nightclubbing in the Lapa district is always undertaken with a lot of skin showing. Especially during *Carnivale.* You need to be nearly naked to capture the true beat of the samba."

Two hours later, Jass decided she hated a know-it-all. As they entered the nightclub and found a table, she could feel Tarik's so-called *true beat* of the samba right through the soles of her shoes. Even with a skin-tight red dress and dangerously high stilettos, she almost felt overdressed inside Carioca da Lapa, one of the Lapa district's pioneering samba clubs and Eltsin's headquarters. People should be naked when experiencing music this sensual.

Looking around, she discovered many people in the club came close to that description. Some women wore shirts made out of thin metal strips with nothing underneath. While other statuesque *mulatas* wearing glittery *Carnivale* garb clung to their partners as if they couldn't stand on their own. Even by glancing twice, Jass would not have been able to swear to the true gender of every woman she saw on the dance floor.

As it turned out, however, it was Tarik who looked overdressed with a lightweight linen jacket covering his sleeveless T-shirt. All the other sweaty young men in the joint were clad only in their undershirts. And as the evening progressed some of those T-shirts had come off in time to the beat. Everyone in the place seemed to have begun their drinking well before noon.

Tarik ordered them the local drink: *cachaca*, sugarcane alcohol tempered with crushed ice, sugar and lime juice. Then he held out his hand. "Couples come to Carioca da Lapa for only one reason, love. Let's check out those samba skills of yours."

She let him pull her into his arms. "I thought we were here to do recon," she whispered. He hugged her tightly against his body as they moved onto the crowded dance floor.

"Oh, but we are. Let's see if anyone here rec-
ognizes Celile and Zohdi." Tarik pulled her
even tighter to him, until she felt completely
surrounded by his masculine presence. Hot and
spicy and full of rigid male power.

The samba in this club played in time to a
reggae beat. Slow. Sensual. Steamy. Keeping
the beat with conga drums, cowbells and primi-
tive sticks that thrummed the music right to her
bones. Tarik began to move, swiveling his hips
like a pro. He took her by the hands and pushed
her an arms' length away. But his eyes locked
onto hers, sending the hypnotic rhythm straight
through her veins by the force of his formidable
gaze.

She felt it in every inch of her body. The
sexual gaze, the heat, the noise. Her nerve endings came alive in a dull burning flame.

Jass had been in a lot of tricky situations
on those missions when she was acting the
part of a girlfriend. But she had never felt

so completely wrapped up in the moment as she did right now. Shaking her head, she tried to throw off the spell of Tarik's personality. This mission should be no different than all the rest—despite her having to work with rogue agent Tarik Kadir. She wouldn't let it get to her.

She tried closing her eyes, but that was little better. She could still smell his virile musk and feel his gaze raking over her body, making her sweat in places no one could see.

He pulled her close again and swung them around. "Your samba act is fine, love," he murmured in her ear. "But your reactions to your lover aren't quite up to the mark. Remember to behave like Celile would on the dance floor with the man she loves. Loosen up."

He was telling her how to behave undercover? How dare this outwardly charming reprobate tell the best undercover operative in the business how to do her job?

Straightening her spine, Jass pulled back and smiled, though she let her eyes tell the truth of what she was feeling. "I've studied the woman for years. Celile Kocak is never loose, *love.*"

She'd gritted out the words so only he could hear. But Tarik's reactions to what she'd said weren't what she'd expected.

He manhandled her back against his chest and plundered her mouth with a kiss that was deep and hard and took her breath away. "I'll bet she comes undone in bed," he whispered against her lips. "Wanna go practice?"

Jass's first reaction was to jerk away in panic, but Tarik held her fast. "Remember your act, darling."

Exasperated, Jass narrowed her eyes at him and spoke in a loud clear voice. "You'll need to excuse me for a moment, darling. I must use the restroom."

Tarik stepped back and opened his arms,

holding up his palms. "Of course, my love. But hurry back. I'll count the minutes."

Swearing under her breath, Jass headed through the throng of dancers toward the back of the club. This was *mission impossible.* But their assignment should've been her salvation, making up for the fumble with the Nigerian.

Instead of her usual feelings of control and being ready for anything, when she moved across the room and looked for a back entry, she felt the solid premonition of doom.

You're one intense little cookie, aren't you? Tough guy. One cool agent. More alpha than most of the men you meet.

That was Jass O'Reilly. Still, Tarik had clearly felt her response to him while he was holding her in his arms. Jass might believe she was invincible and she put on a harsh front, but underneath everything else she was all woman.

The sexual tension had shimmered between them, drawing them together like a magnet. Precisely what he didn't need at this stage in his life. Loyalty to his family called for him to avoid any kind of entanglements during this all important mission.

Stalking back to their table, he kicked back to watch the crowds. But he couldn't keep his mind off of Jass.

She'd flinched when he'd touched her. Flinched like a school girl. And she'd given him a challenging look full of— As he thought about it now, that look in her eyes could've been vulnerability.

That was it, he decided. Jass was tough on the outside to hide a defenseless inside. Like one of those hard-candy-covered chocolates. She was used to taking charge, taking risks alone and getting her orders from only her bosses at the CIA. She wasn't used to anyone challenging that rigid outer shell.

Jass was an excellent operative because she was intelligent and perceptive and had nearly total recall of anything she'd ever read. But she wasn't a team player.

Then again, he didn't need a team on this mission. He hadn't even wanted a partner. But he was willing to bet his life that Jass would step up and do whatever was required to get the job done.

All he had to do was keep his own mind and hands in the game. Easier said than done.

A while later, after ordering his second round of drinks, Tarik realized she'd been gone too long. Was she doing a little side reconnaissance on her own? Or had she run into trouble?

Either way, he'd better quit sitting on his butt daydreaming and find her.

He got to his feet and asked the waitress to direct him to the ladies' room. She threw him a skeptical look but pointed him in the right direction with a small laugh.

Yeah, he would bet she saw a little of everything during *Carnivale.*

Tarik thanked her and made his way through the tangle of sweaty, dancing bodies all moving to a bossa nova beat. In a darkened corner of the main floor, he found a staircase to the penthouse above. He made a mental note of its placement but moved on into an alcove that held what was loosely called the public restrooms.

The alcove was crowded with lines of people waiting for a turn at the toilets. He thought about asking someone to check the stalls for Jass but decided against it. No telling who was a real patron of the club and who was here on some kind of criminal business.

As he stood toward the rear of the lines considering his next move, he heard footsteps on the stairs behind him. An argument reached his ears, and he had just enough time to duck for cover under the open stairwell. The conversation was taking place in the Taj Zabbar language and the two men speaking were making no attempt to keep their voices down.

They stopped on the landing right above his head to continue their disagreement. "I do not like the idea of staying in the country for the next four days, Excellency. It is not safe. Too much frivolity in this place."

"Nonsense." With that one word, Tarik recognized the second speaker's deep voice. "The Russian...uh...Eltsin is a powerful man. He will protect us while we are in Brazil. Has he not already told the elder that we have no risk of losing anything in this little charade of his?"

"But what about the other bidders? I am concerned about our main mission and the other item. The one we were sent to Rio to claim."

"Remember your place and trust me to do what needs to be done. We've been invited to stay for the next few days at Eltsin's retreat in the mountains not far from here. I assume that he means for us to procure that other item during our private stay. His men will escort us into the mountains tomorrow. In the meantime, let's enjoy ourselves, shall we?"

"Yes, Excellency. Whatever you say."

Tarik recognized the more formidable voice as that of Malik Kasim Taj Zabbar, head of the secret police in Zabbarán. The two men lit cigars and proceeded down the stairs, disappearing into the crowds on the dance floor.

Well, that answered one thing for sure. The Taj Zabbar were here in Rio to attend Eltsin's auction. But now Tarik had many more questions. What charade? And what was the other item they'd been talking about?

And where the devil was Jass?

A commotion erupted above his head. He heard a man growling orders in Portuguese.

And he heard a woman's voice, calm and cool, returning the sentiments in Russian.

Jass. Tarik shot up the stairs without thinking. What had she gotten herself into?

Chapter 5

Jass tried to keep her voice down, low and sultry like Celile would. But this idiot body-guard didn't speak any of her languages and he wouldn't give in and take her to see the Russian. All he wanted to do was flash his knife and make threats in a slang version of Portuguese.

All *she'd* wanted to do was a little scouting around. Maybe get a line on what the upcoming auction was all about. And she'd hoped to do so unnoticed. No such luck.

Now she was going to have to use force to make the bodyguard let her go. Something she was sure Celile would never be caught dead doing. Ah well.

Flipping her head and allowing the annoying silky veil of fake long hair to fall over one eye, she aimed a come-hither look at him. She continued to work her womanly wiles as she reached for the hem of her dress and slowly began lifting it up her thighs.

The bodyguard's eyes bugged out of his head and his tongue nearly hit the floor. A little farther and Jass could reach the derringer she'd holstered between her thighs and right below her crotch. Another inch and...

"Trouble, love?" Tarik came up behind the bodyguard and pulled him into a headlock before the guy ever knew what had hit him.

One neat karate chop to the forearm and the guy's knife disappeared into the darkness. Next

Tarik used a tricky pressure-point move, and in seconds the bodyguard was quietly laid out unconscious on the floor.

Jass dropped her dress and shook her head. "I was handling it, Kadir. No sense making anyone mad."

Tarik's expression went hard. Something in his gaze shook her. But she didn't have time to consider it.

He took her by the wrist and spun them both in the direction of the stairs. "Tell me later. Right now, I need to make a quick exit before the Taj Zabbar spot me in the crowd."

"The Taj are here? Tonight?" She had seen two Middle Eastern men leaving the penthouse suite as she was hiding down the hall. They were the Taj Zabbar? Couldn't prove it by her.

"Can we *please* discuss this later?" He hustled her down the stairs and pushed through the crowded lines waiting to use the restrooms and mingling around the back exit.

Next thing she knew they were shoving past another couple of sleazy-looking characters who might've been bouncers as Tarik shoved their way out into the alley behind the club. The balmy night air and the unfortunate but prevalent smells of garbage hit her smack in the face.

"Keep moving." Tarik dropped her hand and pulled a phone out of his pocket. "We'll have our driver pick us up around the block."

Yeah, if we live that long. "Hold on a minute. Let me reach my weapon, before…"

Tarik elbowed her in the back and propelled her forward as he frantically poked buttons on his phone. "Keep moving if you want to stay alive."

Of all the arrogant, testosterone-loaded—

Jass didn't waste any breath telling him off as she pounded down the dark cobblestones in her stilettos. Not yet. First she needed to live through the rest of this night.

But afterward…rogue agent Tarik Kadir had better watch his step. She was ready to let him have it.

By the time they arrived back at the honeymoon suite, Jass was in a full snit as she stormed into the bathroom and slammed the door behind her. A tiny kernel of guilt snuck up on Tarik. As annoying as she had been on the ride home, he was still hyperaware of that vulnerability he'd spotted in her on the dance floor.

He could see how CIA covert officer Jasmine O'Reilly would be hard-pressed to accept help from anyone in the middle of an assignment. Even if it might save both her life and the mission. Irritating. And yet, Tarik also found it somehow endearing.

But he hadn't expected the private side of Jass O'Reilly to be so sexy. And a world-class kisser to boot.

The two of them still needed to arrive at a better working relationship. A good, soul-revealing conversation was in order. But not tonight. Tonight he would back off and let her lick her wounded pride.

He stepped into the walk-in bedroom closet, where the hotel valets had hung their things, and began pulling out a change of clothes for himself. The bathroom door opened and Jass walked out, completely covered in one of the hotel's full-length terry robes. She still wore Celile's hair and makeup, but in the robe she was all Jass. A little sweet and hesitant. And a whole lot spicy.

"I'll take the couch, Kadir. Give me a moment to gather up a pillow and blanket."

"No can do," he told her with a shrug. "If any of the hotel staff lets themselves in to make up the kitchen or bring in an early breakfast, it won't be acceptable for the lovebirds to be sleeping in separate rooms."

For a split second she looked terrified. He had a guilty feeling that she was remembering the supposedly fake kiss he'd given her on the dance floor. He was having some trouble forgetting the kiss himself.

He reached for a solution that would give them both space. "You take the bed. There's a decent chaise on the balcony terrace right outside the bedroom. I'll be good out there. Give me a minute to shower."

He edged around her as she stood mute where she was. "It'll be fine, partner. Don't worry. I sleep like a rock."

It was a lie; he seldom needed more than a couple hours a night and always slept lightly in case of attack. But the excuse was the best he could come up with on short notice. The one thing he hadn't lied about was that she needn't worry. As much as she turned him on in so many ways, he wouldn't be rushing into a sexual relationship in the middle of an undercover assignment. Not with anyone, and least of all not with the woman who'd flinched in response to his touch and whose kiss was one of the most sensual and memorable of his lifetime.

Restless and too warm, Jass tossed the covers for the umpteenth time that night and sat up in bed. She automatically turned her head to glance toward the sliding glass doors leading to the balcony terrace, making sure Tarik was still where he'd been the last seven times she'd checked during the long night.

But this time when she looked, the chaise was empty. She spotted him then, standing with his back to her at the railing, staring out at the first rays of the rising sun.

Her body seemed to react to the sight of him all on its own. She swung her legs over the side of the king-size bed and threw open the glass doors, moving in his direction without fully knowing why.

He had to have heard her sliding back the doors, but he didn't turn and remained silent and brooding where he stood. She went to the railing too and gazed out on beautiful Copacabana Beach and beyond that across the bay to Sugarloaf Mountain shrouded in the morning mists.

Tarik didn't turn but said, "It's early. Go back to bed."

She gazed up at his profile. "I was hot and needed some air."

He said nothing more and made no move. She wanted to drag her gaze away, but couldn't keep herself from staring at his hard jawline and rigid stance. He wasn't wearing a shirt and his broad muscular chest led down to a flat belly and lower to a pair of white boxer shorts. The purely masculine and sensual sight captured her attention and imagination, paralyzing her with sudden longing.

She'd always known Tarik Kadir as the covert officer to play the part of a ladies' man. The charmer. The agent who could worm his way inside any nest of bad guys with a few glib words and a smile.

Not her type. Not even someone she could be friends with, really.

Still, her body had reacted almost violently to his kiss last night. She'd been hyper-aware of the extraordinary strength in the arms that held her tight. Super sensitive to his calloused fingers as he'd touched the skin on her arms. And extremely susceptible to the warmth of his breath on her neck. It had so affected her that she'd run like a scared rabbit.

Inside, where all her insecurities lay, she was still running.

She thought of later last night, when there'd also been that strange way his eyes had held hers for a single moment after he'd come to her rescue. Something she saw in those dark eyes said there might be more to the man. Could it be that all his fast-talking charm hid a sensitive and intelligent person underneath?

She looked at him again. As the first rays of sun hit his face, the strong set of his chin made her want to reassess all of her initial impressions. Perhaps she and her handler Ed had rushed to judgment about Tarik.

"So," she began. "You went into Zabbarán to help your brother and found a nuclear reactor. That must've been a shock."

"Not especially." He turned and looked at her for the first time that morning. "By then I would've expected anything from the Taj. Both my brothers have firsthand knowledge of how truly terrifying the Taj tribe can behave when no one is watching."

"Tell me about them— Your family, I mean."

Tarik went to the chaise and sat, patting the

spot beside him and inviting her to join him on the wide cushions. "Not much to tell. Darin and Shakir and their new wives are everything to me. I'm the baby of our three brothers. But there's also dozens of cousins and relations and now a new nephew and another baby on the way. We're a tight group, though some of the rest of our family are spread all over the world."

"How has such an extended family managed to stay close together when you have no homeland?" Jass did settle on the chaise, but she kept a good distance between their two bodies and folded her arms tightly across her chest, her legs up under her butt.

No sense giving her own wayward body any ideas.She was curious about him and his family. About how he'd turned into the man he'd become. That's all there was to this sudden need to be close.

"Ah. Well, we're raised with a deep sense of family loyalty. It's tradition with the Kadirs.

But even that didn't always keep us physically close."

He stopped talking, took a breath and glanced over at her. "Are you cold? You don't have much on. Just that T-shirt. You want to go inside or maybe grab your robe?"

"I'm fine. It's quite balmy out here." Again she was grateful for her olive complexion keeping the blush from her cheeks, but she wasn't ready to open her arms or unfold her legs from beneath her body.

Tarik gave her an odd look, but then clasped his hands and leaned his elbows on his knees. "When the family first realized we were being threatened by the Taj Zabbar, they called us all to a family conclave from our various corners of the world. Darin had been running Kadir Shipping from a Greek island. Shakir had resigned his commission from a British paratrooper regiment in Afghanistan and was in the process of starting up his own security business. And I…well, you know where I was."

She nodded but wasn't sure he saw the movement since he was staring at the floor. "Every one of you dropped your lives and came, without question?"

"It's that loyalty thing again. Runs in the family. Identity and loyalty have been a huge part of our makeup for centuries." He stared down at his joined fingers. "Besides, I would go anywhere for my two brothers. I would die for them. They kept me going when things were rough."

"What about your parents?"

He sighed, not so loud that she was supposed to hear, but she noticed anyway. "Our mother died of cancer when I was young. It shook all of us, but especially my father. He left us with the help and dived into his businesses with his complete attention.

"Turns out, the *help* left a lot to be desired,"

he added with a snicker. "Oh, we were fed and clothed. But all three of us were very young and had been completely spoiled by our mother. None of us knew how to grieve and we were blindsided by the loss of our parents' love."

He shrugged and seemed to struggle for the right words. She was willing to bet that he seldom faced these old memories. They seemed to be raising a range of emotions he didn't know how to handle.

"I'm sorry," she said to fill up the silence. "I know how bad that must have been. My mother died when I was about ten. It was a difficult thing to get past."

But her mother had not been the type to spoil her, not in the least. In fact, Jass remembered a moment when she'd felt almost glad her mother was gone, enabling her to be alone with her easygoing father.

However, things hadn't exactly worked out that way either.

Tarik frowned and turned his head toward her. "Yes, it was bad enough. Did your father take up the slack in your life after losing your mother?"

"He would've liked to. But he had to work to support us. And his job with the CIA suddenly became all about the covert assignments and he was gone most of the time. My mother's family took up the slack, as you call it."

Tarik chuckled. "You should see your face. Like you tasted something sour. I'm guessing your mother's family wasn't exactly what you had in mind."

Jass chuckled at her own reactions to the memories. "Um…no. They were immigrants from Iran and very strict. They expected me to grieve all the time for the first year. I was only ten. After that, it was pray, pray, pray. I escaped during breaks and in the summers when my dad was between assignments."

She tried to push the memories aside like she

always had as a child. It wasn't working as well this time.

"Did you do anything else to escape?"

"Like what? I did read a lot. And I day-dreamed about having adventures with my father. I idolized him." When she noticed Tarik's expression began to change again, she shifted the focus back to him. "So what did you do to escape?"

"Me? I made up stories and acted them out." He stood and paced along the length of the ter-race. "In my daydreams, I became anything I wanted. I could go anywhere in my mind that I wanted—be anyone I wanted. A pirate, a cowboy or an astronaut. I learned I could escape into my head anytime if I plastered a smile on my face and stayed quiet."

The man was a romantic. She never would've guessed that about him. Knowing it now, know-ing he understood her daydreams, made him seem more human. Someone she could build a friendship with after this mission was over.

They were both quiet for a few minutes while Tarik kept pacing. She suspected he was as lost in his thoughts as she'd been.

"Seems we have a few things in common." The sympathy in her voice astounded even her.

Tarik stepped behind the chaise and gently laid his two hands on her shoulders. It was a friendly gesture, but the electric shock that sizzled between them caused her to draw back in surprise.

"Tense?" He began kneading her neck muscles. "You need to relax with me. I thought we were getting closer to developing a decent working relationship. We'll never pull off being lovers if you keep flinching every time we touch."

She jerked away from his hands and stood to face him. "I can pull off any covert op. Don't worry about me—I'm the best you've ever worked with. Keep your hands to yourself when we're alone and stick to your job."

"Jass…" He held out his hands, palms up, as if pleading for her understanding. "Before we're through with this mission, we may need to be seen touching and kissing while in public places. And it's even possible we may have to sleep in the same bed. We'd better come up with some solution if this thing between us is going to be a problem."

Tarik looked exasperated but went on, "Maybe what we need is a good old-fashioned roll in the hay. To break the ice. It might conquer your inhibitions."

Speechless for a moment, Jass stared until her indignation came pouring out. "Not on your li—"

"Ms. Kocak. Sheik Zohdi." A male voice coming behind a knock on the door to the sitting room had both her and Tarik racing into the bedroom for their weapons. "I've brought your breakfast. Courtesy of Chef Langdon. Please to join me?"

Chef Langdon? As in Ed, her handler? Jass reached for her robe instead of the Glock and nodded to Tarik to don his robe, too.

She'd never been more glad in her whole life for an untimely interruption.

By the time Tarik drew on his robe and opened the bedroom door, the supposed waiter had set aside his breakfast tray and was standing on the dining table checking out the chandelier. The fellow turned out to be Bosque, the Rio CIA station chief they'd met yesterday.

The guy had a disturbing way of turning up at the oddest times. He was beginning to get on Tarik's nerves.

Bosque had one of those high-tech bug-detection devices in his hand. When he saw Tarik, the station chief raised his other hand to indicate Tarik shouldn't say anything until he was through with his check.

Jass came out of the bedroom right behind Tarik and stood silently while they waited. She had her arms protectively folded over her chest again, and Tarik would bet she was wishing she'd never come out on the terrace to confront him.

That made two of them. He was still battling the coil of longing that had settled in his gut from touching her. But their situation was becoming intolerable. They needed to find a way past whatever discord lay between them.

The more he considered it, the better he liked his bright idea. They should have a quickie fling. Get past all the sexual tension and get on with their mission.

"Looks clean," Bosque said as he jumped down from the table. "Langdon's in town. And we have a couple of messages for you."

Bosque held out the hand with the bug

detector. "Here, Kadir. Keep this device and check for bugs wherever and whenever you think it's necessary. Run over this room periodically."

"You believe Eltsin will listen in or record the Messenger and her sheik lover? Why?"

The station chief shrugged a shoulder. "Maybe Eltsin. Maybe your Taj Zabbar friends. The whole lot of them are paranoid as hell." He turned to the breakfast tray, pulled off a large white tablecloth and placed it over the table. "Help yourselves to coffee or açaí berry juice, while I give you the rest of Langdon's instructions."

Tarik opted for coffee while Jass picked up a toasted baguette with melted cheese and popped it in her mouth. He debated having the papaya but decided against it. He'd lost his appetite on the terrace earlier.

"We're not getting anywhere on figuring out what the item that's up for bid will be,"

Bosque told them. "But we have our ears to the ground. You can bet someone in the Brazilian criminal community has heard what's for sale. Particularly if it has something to do with nuclear weapons. You can't keep that kind of thing quiet."

Jass nodded and lounged in one of the dining chairs. Bosque joined her at the table. Tarik decided to remain standing. At the moment he was full of left-over nervous energy, enough to power his own nuclear weapons.

"Langdon wants you two to check in periodically with him. He's setting up a Fruti Vita stand on the beach and expects your first rendezvous this afternoon." He cleared his throat. "We're working on a plan to get you inside Eltsin's mountain retreat early. Maybe you can gather more info there."

Tarik didn't like the idea of working blindfolded. "Does the Task Force know the Taj Zabbar are already here?"

Bosque stared for a moment, then shook his head. "I have men taking pictures of everyone coming and going from the club. But there's hundreds of photos to go through. You're sure it was the Taj?"

"Definitely. I ran into a couple of them last night at the club. A man in a tux with another man dressed in a black suit. They shouldn't be too hard to spot inside that casual nightclub."

"I'll get someone on it. Meanwhile—" Bosque reached into his jacket pocket and withdrew two pairs of sunglasses. "Here. Each of you wear these at all times, even at night if possible."

Jass took hers and flipped them over, studying them in her hands. "What are these? They feel weighted."

"Signaling devices," Bosque told her. "Here, let me show you."

He stood over Jass and showed her how to slide the side piece forward. "Doing that sends us an alarm, along with your GPS coordinates. If you practice, you can do it surreptitiously without taking them off." Bosque bent close and eased the glasses onto her face. "Like this."

Tarik felt his blood pressure soar when the station chief touched Jass's face. A green haze clouded his vision.

Geez, get over yourself, Kadir.

He didn't know which would become the bigger danger on this mission. The Taj Zabbar, or the tempting woman who was now his partner.

Chapter 6

Heading for the beach, Jass darted across the boulevard in front of the hotel with Tarik in her wake. Damned man hadn't let her out of his sight all morning. She understood his possessive act was in keeping with Zohdi's character. But sometimes he laid that act on a little thick in private and it was beginning to feel all too realistic.

She was having trouble decoding her true feelings for Tarik. On the one hand, they had a few things in common. He was a dreamer and good at being a chameleon on the job. But she only wished she knew for sure when he was acting and when he was being himself.

He also seemed to have as strong a sense of loyalty as did she, though his was to his family and hers was to her country. Logically they should be able to develop a relationship based on those few facts alone.

Still, on the other hand, a couple of things about him continued to bother her. She had relied on Ed's opinions for most of her adult life. Her handler had saved her back end more times than she could count and was nearly always right. Ed remained unconvinced that Tarik was one of the good guys.

Then there was the matter of that nagging physical tug-of-war between them whenever Tarik got too close. When he touched her, those old reliable gut instincts of hers kept screaming to run away from him before he pulled her into something that was bigger than she could handle.

Frustrated and wishing she could make a decision about him and get on with their mission, she came to the conclusion Tarik may have been right about one thing this morning. Maybe what they needed was a quickie fling. *Slam bam, thank you, ma'am.* It wasn't her style. She didn't do sex for sex's sake. Yet, she needed to step out of her comfort zone with him somehow in order to get over her jitters.

This assignment was too important to her career to let a little thing like being sexually uptight ruin it.

Hanging on to the brim of her straw hat in the wind, Jass tried to act casual as she strolled the colorful and wide pavement at the edge of Copacabana Beach. She could feel Tarik walking right behind her and her nerves kept jangling with mixed messages.

He was safe and familiar. He was mysterious and a complete stranger.

She gritted her teeth as she searched for Ed's Fruti Vita stand. Seeing her handler should help calm her down and put things in perspective.

"Do we have any idea where this juice stand is supposedly located?" Tarik came up next to her and whispered in her ear so no one else could hear.

Turning to him, Jass opened her mouth to speak, but the mere sight of him in the bright sunshine struck her dumb. He was stunning. Handsome and virile enough to make her weak in the knees. In his lightweight suit, panama hat and the aviator sunglasses that Bosque had supplied, he looked every bit the part of a larger-than-life Middle Eastern terrorist.

"Uh...uh..." She bit her tongue to keep from stuttering and tried to rein her anxiety. "No. Keep looking. It has to be up here on the beach close by."

The beach seemed almost deserted for the middle of the afternoon during *Carnivale* weekend. A few bikini-clad women sunbathers snoozed on blankets here and there, and she thought she spotted a volleyball game starting up a hundred yards down the beach. Everyone else must be napping or resting up for the night's festivities.

She took a couple more steps and found herself absently fanning her face with her hand. "It's really scorching hot on the beach today, isn't it?"

Tarik was staring out over the huge expanse of beach sand and didn't turn. "February is the hottest month in the southern hemisphere. But I noticed you still look cool and in control. Celile would be proud of you."

Jass didn't feel cool or in control next to Tarik. Not in the least. And the last thing she cared about today was what Celile would think. Celile would probably screw him and get on with her life. But that wasn't something Jass could jump into as easily as she'd learned to shoot a gun.

"The bay is a beautiful deep green today," Tarik suddenly announced in the phony half accent of Sheik Zohdi. "Pretty, though different from the blue Mediterranean we love, yes? Nice day for a beach stroll. But I'm becoming thirsty."

She threw him a look of utter frustration, wondering what the hell he thought he was doing. But as she turned, she spotted a line of wooden stands right ahead on the sand at the edge of the sidewalk pavement.

"Oh, yes, I agree. Let's see if we can find a Fruti Vita stand that's open." She marched out onto the brilliant white sand and headed down the line of stands.

Most of the food and drink stands were closed down for the afternoon. They'd probably been jumping during the morning what with the tourists in town for *Carnivale.* This afternoon in the heat everyone seemed to be taking a break until the evening parades began and their customers returned.

She'd about given up on finding the right one when she darted around the last stand and found her handler there in disguise as the juice vendor. Immediately, Jass felt a bit more stable than she had only a moment ago.

"Everything under control?" Ed asked.

Before she could respond, Tarik came up beside her. "Isn't this spot too wide open for a meeting?"

Ed nodded his head and closed the wooden flap on the front of the stand, shutting them out. A moment later he opened a side door and shuffled them both into the tiny, sweltering space inside the booth.

"This suit you better, Kadir?"

Tarik's eyes went cold in the heat, but he said nothing.

Ed scowled at him, though when he turned to her, it was with a smile. "Still no word on what's for sale this week. But we've come up with a new plan for finding out. Tonight is the first of the *Carnivale* parades and the first of the Samba schools' competitions. A good chance to obtain intel unnoticed."

"What competitions?" Jass wasn't sure she understood.

"The whole purpose of the street parades is for local samba schools to compete with rival schools to win the title of best school of the year." When she still looked confused, he continued, "It's a big frigging deal with all the locals in Rio. Tonight the samba school that Eltsin's *bicheiro* controls will have its first shot at a parade entry. He'll have no choice but to attend."

"I get it," Tarik chimed in soberly. "While he and most of his men are gone, we break in to his offices and see if we can find out what's coming up for auction."

"Right." Ed reached under the counter and hauled up a designer, satchel-style handbag. "The Task Force lent us a few high-tech toys to assist…"

"I don't like it." Tarik interrupted him and turned to her. "Neither of us is an expert in breaking into computers and that's where our best shot of finding info in his office would be. There isn't a chance in hell of us stumbling over the item itself during a B & E attempt."

"True, the item is no doubt at Eltsin's mountain retreat," Ed agreed, taking back control of the conversation. "But the techs came up with some toys that will make your jobs in his office easier. I know Jass at least can become an expert with only a few minutes of instruction."

Ed hesitated, seemingly watching for Tarik's facial responses. But Tarik's face had become a mask of serious intent. Not even a hint of his usual grin was anywhere to be seen.

"Look, Kadir." Ed's tone changed all of a sudden as he spoke casually to Tarik. "Why don't I give these toys and the instructions to Jass while you contact your brothers? A Darin Kadir has been calling the Task Force and is anxious to speak to you. Is it true that you have an encrypted satellite phone that you can use?"

Tarik nodded sharply in response. "Fine. I'd like to see what Kadir intel has come up with anyway. I'll step out on the beach where I can get a better signal and still keep watch in case anyone is within earshot." He turned to Jass. "Take his instructions but don't agree to anything until you talk to me. I'll be back in a few minutes."

Jass's temper flared for a split second. But almost immediately after he was out the door, she decided Tarik was being a good partner and not trying to run the show.

Ed, it seemed, was not quite as generous. "What's he been up to, anyway? Has he been trying to convince you to do something you're not comfortable doing?"

"No, Ed," she lied. "We're learning to become friends. For the sake of the mission. That's all."

No sense enflaming Ed any further. Jass would make up her own mind whether she and Tarik would become anything more than friends and partners.

"Don't try to be friends with a snake, little girl. If you try, the guy will only let you down," he warned her. "You might find yourself involved in something that could be a career-ender or something even worse—like a life-ender. Stay away from him."

Ed sure disliked Tarik. Jass could sort of understand his hesitance to trust a man who'd quit the Task Force and was heading up his own covert operation doing heaven knows what. But…

"Ed, I have to be his partner. It's in the job description. How can I play his girlfriend and still stay away from him?"

Ed pulled off his ball cap and ran a hand over the bald spot underneath. "You're a pro. You can pull off anything. I care too much about you to see anything happen to your career." He sighed. "I do trust you, Jass. But be careful."

How could she resist when he was so concerned for her welfare?

Trying to calm his fears for her, she cooed, "I will. And I am the pro here. You know I can watch out for myself. Don't worry about me."

"I can't help worrying." Ed took a deep breath and shook his head. "But okay, for now we have work to do. Let me show you how to use these gadgets and then suggest a plan for tonight. You can run rings around that Kadir guy. But don't forget what I said."

How could she forget? Every second of this mission seemed consumed with nothing but thoughts of Tarik Kadir. Something was going to have to give soon.

She only hoped she wouldn't be the one to break first.

Tarik swallowed down his annoyance over the handler's remarks as his brother Darin picked up the call.

"Can you talk?" Darin asked.

Tarik threw a quick glance at his surroundings as he adjusted his covert earpiece. He stood near the shore on a particularly isolated stretch of beach. The nearest person was a nearly nude woman, sunbathing about a hundred yards away. He wasn't worried about anyone trying to listen in to his conversation unseen, because Kadir phones all had special encryption coding.

"Yeah. I'm good. What have you discovered?"

"We've made a couple of good initial contacts

in the criminal community around Rio. I have one particularly solid lead who claims Tuesday's auction is about nuclear fissionable material." He hesitated. "But the informant also said some of the same things you overheard last night. Everyone in the know there in Brazil is aware the whole deal is a sham. Seems it's only the American Task Force and the local CIA who're supposed to believe that's what this meeting is all about."

"Do we have any idea what's really going on?"

"Not yet." Darin sounded as though he had something more to say.

Tarik waited, knowing his brother would eventually get to whatever was concerning him.

Finally Darin cleared his throat and began. "Cousin Karim asked if you had a thumbnail drive and wireless transmitter and if you know how to use it to transmit the data back to us."

"I know how to use them in a pinch. You want me to try accessing Eltsin's computer system?"

"Perhaps. If you have the opportunity and the access to the equipment. But my guess is the computer we want will not be located in his main offices. Eltsin is street smart. He would keep this kind of info close. In a laptop or a BlackBerry he carries around with him."

"Right. I'll see what I can do." It was now Tarik's turn to ask a tricky question. "What's your best guess, brother? Do you think this whole charade is for our benefit as much as for the Task Force? Is it possible Eltsin has gotten word the Kadirs are close and is waiting to ambush us somehow? The Taj secret police officer I ran into last night seemed overly confident when I overheard his conversation."

It took a moment for Darin to answer. "All things are possible. Shakir is on his way and we're putting together a stealth backup team to help with surveillance at Eltsin's fortress in the mountains. Give us a little time to see what we can come up with." Skepticism filled his voice. "I can't quite buy that Eltsin is partnering with the Taj, but we'll wait and see. In the meantime, watch your back."

Tarik thanked his brother, bid him goodbye and headed for the handler's Fruti Vita stand. He always watched his back. The trouble on this mission was centered more around keeping his eyes off his beautiful partner's back long enough to keep them both alive.

He knocked once and entered, finding Jass in the process of kissing her handler's cheek in a much too intimate manner. Jealousy ran through his mind.

Hell. What the devil was he thinking? Jealousy was out of bounds. She was his partner, not his lover.

Besides, this mission was all about the Taj Zabbar and their nuclear ambitions. Not about his partner.

Jass looked up at him with those big brown eyes of Celile's. "Glad you're back. I was getting set to take off." She patted the purse under her arm. "I have toys and instructions. And we need to go get fitted for our costumes before it gets any later."

"Costumes?"

She scooted past him and stepped out into the humid sunshine. "I'll tell you all about it after we pick up our car."

"Car?"

Jass laughed. "Come on…I've got it covered. Thanks again, Ed." She headed up the beach.

Tarik turned to follow her, but Ed's voice stopped him. "Just a second, Kadir."

He held fast at the threshold and glared at Jass's handler. "Yeah?"

"I don't know what game you think you're playing by horning in on the Task Force and taking over this mission, but I'm keeping my eyes on you. Jass is my responsibility and if you hurt her in any way, you're a dead man."

Tarik's fingers ground into the wooden door-jamb. "Without me, there would be no mission and you know it."

Ed glared at him but said nothing.

"But I've got a question for you." Tarik held his ground and quirked a brow. "Wouldn't this mission proceed perfectly well using Bosque, the station chief, as a standby go-between from the Task Force to us? Why is it necessary for a big-shot CIA officer to do the actual legwork?"

"I'm only here because of Jass," Ed grumbled. "Bosque is supposed to be a good man. But this assignment may make or break Jass's advancement. Nothing can go wrong."

Tarik didn't think that was a good enough answer, but he let it pass until he could talk to Jass. "Nothing will go wrong if you let us do the work we're paid to do. Trust your own operative to do the right thing. I'll watch out for her."

"She means a lot to me."

Tarik could suddenly see the man had real fatherly feelings for his operative. Ed wore his emotions on his sleeve when it came to Jass O'Reilly.

"Watch your back, Kadir."

Yeah, that was the second time in less than ten minutes he'd been given the same warning. But as he walked out into the afternoon sun and stepped across the smooth, white sand, Tarik figured it wasn't that his back needed watching. No, it was his raging libido that was giving him the biggest problem.

"This costume is outrageous." Tarik squirmed in the passenger seat of their tiny dark green sedan. "Why did you ever agree to anything this juvenile for Sheik Zohdi?"

"I think you look adorable. And a pirate

costume is not juvenile. It's dashing." Unlike her costume, which at the moment was giving her fits. "Besides, under that *gia-normous* hat and the eye patch, no one would ever recognize Zohdi. Relax. We're not out to win any awards, but to blend in."

Tarik gave her one of his charmer-style looks. "As a matter of fact, I happen to be a big fan of *your* costume. You pick that out?"

The sparkly red bodysuit clung to her skin like a dive suit. Not a speck of bare skin showed from her neck to her ankles. Yet after she'd put the thing on, she felt sexier than ever before in her life.

"No, I didn't pick out either of our costumes. But at least mine is far better than all those sparkly thong getups we've been seeing on the streets."

"I'd give a lot to see you in one of those *getups*. But some other time. That much skin wouldn't be quite the right thing for Celile."

"Keep your mind on the mission, Kadir."

He chuckled and turned to look out the windshield. "Tell me again why you have to drive?"

"Sheik Zohdi does not drive. He's chauffeured everywhere he travels. You're not worried about my driving skills, are you?"

Tarik raised a shoulder. "No. Not unless we run into real trouble."

"Well, I wasn't planning on running into trouble tonight. Are you?"

"You never know," he retorted. "I'm not crazy about the whole idea of going back to Eltsin's offices tonight. It doesn't feel right."

"Why not? Everyone should be on the streets watching the samba parade."

Tarik folded his arms over his chest as she stopped for a traffic cop. "Maybe. But I can't believe we'll find any useful intel here without having to fight our way out. No one with any sense leaves sensitive info unguarded."

"I have a few tricks to use in case we run into security problems. Don't worry."

By the time they found a guarded parking spot a few blocks away and Jass wrestled her heavy feathered headdress onto her head, the area seemed deserted. Instead of blending in to the crowds, the two of them looked ridiculous sneaking down the darkened alleyways.

Tarik echoed her sentiments. "I'm thinking we could do better if we both lose the headgear. You with me?"

They found an empty water barrel and stashed the feathers, the oversized pirate's hat and the fake swashbuckler's sword. "We can pick these up on the way back."

"Hmm." Tarik didn't seem thrilled with the idea.

When they arrived at the nightclub, they found guards at every entrance.

"Time for one of those toys you were issued?"

She elbowed past him and sidestepped around

to the side of the building. The structure was only two stories tall on this side. And no one was guarding the alley with its lack of entrances and no windows.

"You planning on walking through the walls?" he asked with a smirk in his voice. "Those must be some high-tech toys you've got there."

"How're your mountain-climbing skills, Kadir?" She reached into her bag and pulled out what appeared in the darkness to be a flare gun. "This baby will get us inside in moments."

She nearly laughed at his incredulous look as she fired in the air. With a tiny, shallow sounding pop, the titanium grappling hook deployed and struck the tiled roof, embedding itself deep and tight. Carbon fiber threads parachuted back toward them. With another small click, she clipped an aluminum ascender to the bottom of the thread and gestured to Tarik that it was for his foot.

"A little like *Mission Impossible* and James Bond," she murmured. "I love it. Up you go. Send it back down for me."

He looked at the contraption in the shadowed light from the street lamp. "Oh, crap. You're not serious. I hate rooftops and ledges. Can't we find another way?"

"Sure. You can stay here and guard our backs. I'll handle this op alone."

"Not on your life." Tarik pulled off the fake eye patch and rubbed his hands against his black slacks. "Let me worry about my own back. And I'll be guarding your back from right behind you, my love. Lead the way."

Chapter 7

Tarik managed to step off the tile roof and ease inside a second-story window right behind Jass without breaking his neck. Though he didn't like any part of this op, he was determined to keep up with her.

Nothing moved in the darkness of Eltsin's penthouse offices, but the smell of violence lingered in the air. What had happened inside these rooms earlier tonight?

Jass didn't seem to notice the odd sensations he was receiving and it was too dark to see anything more than shadows. She nudged his arm and crept off into the ominous black emptiness, undeterred from her mission. Tarik stood his ground for a second and listened. The sounds of a wall clock and the whir of an electric motor in the distance were all he could hear. Nothing he could put his finger on as out of place, and no hint of human activity he could sense.

Following Jass through what appeared to be a sparsely furnished sitting room, he noted they were passing a darkened alley-style kitchen and a bathroom. Apparently she was looking for computers or file cabinets and nothing else. But the farther into the apartment they traveled, the more Tarik wanted to flick on a light and study his surroundings a bit more thoroughly. Every cell in his body tensed with concern.

Convinced that this was some kind of ambush, he caught up to Jass as she entered the first office space she came to. "Hold on." He stopped her with a firm grip to her forearm. "I think we need to get out of here. Something isn't right."

She quietly removed his fingers by using her own gloved hand. "Nonsense. We're in and no one's around. This won't take me five minutes. Why don't you look in the next room while I break into the computer?"

Their whispered conversation seemed to echo off the walls. This was all wrong.

Too easy.

Jass sat in front of a desk computer and turned a penlight on to study the drive box. Her light was bright enough for Tarik to see that the room was totally vacant of any other furnishings besides the desk and the lone computer. No, not right at all.

He backed out the door and into the hall. Reaching into his inside pocket, he pulled out a set of night-vision goggles and slipped them over his eyes to leave his hands free. No question, he had to give the place a more thorough visual check. And he'd better do it fast.

Moving quickly, he opened each of the other doors off the hall. Nothing but empty rooms and a lone disheveled cot. No filing cabinets, conference tables or office machines. What was going on?

Retracing his steps, Tarik went back toward the sitting room. He stuck his head into the bathroom. Again, nothing. Then he turned to the kitchen and moved far enough into it to check out the whole space.

What was that, lying on the...? Damn. He nudged the object with his booted toe and found what he'd expected. A dead body.

At that exact moment he also caught the unmistakable sounds of police sirens in the distance. Great. They were being set up. But by whom? And why?

Swinging around, he made his way back to Jass in record time. She was on her way out the door of the office. He caught a smug look on her face.

"Got it," she crowed. "Found several computer files on fissionable nuclear material. We've got…"

"Shussh. Listen. Hear that?" He grabbed her by the arm and pulled her through the darkness toward the window where they'd entered a few minutes ago. "Move!"

Two steps later and the sounds of sirens were unmistakable.

"What's happening? Those can't be for us."

"We've been set up. Dead body in the kitchen." They reached the window "Out. Now!"

Jass was a smart enough operative to stop questioning and slip out into the night air without another sound. She crept along the tile roof, not waiting to make sure Tarik was behind her. But he was. He didn't let a botched job deter him from being her protector.

Determined to stand at her back regardless of what happened next, he dove out the window and caught up to her in a few seconds. Shouts were coming from the street below, and the sirens were still shrieking through the noisy night.

Jass was about to crawl over the ledge when she threw a quick glance down to the blind alley where they'd begun their flight. "Eltsin's goons," she whispered and pointed below. "We'll have to find another way."

"Whatever we do, we'd better do it soon. The cops will be here any second."

She looked uncertain. As though this change of plans was so unexpected that she'd been thrown off track.

He imagined she would snap out of it any moment and come up with a backup escape plan. She was a pro and the best operative he knew. But he didn't wait to find out for sure.

"This way." He swung around and headed

back up to the roof and then to the other side of the building. He crouched low to avoid being seen from below.

"That's the way to the side street," Jass said in a stage whisper. "A guard was there when we first entered."

Tarik kept going. "Maybe not anymore."

Sure enough, as they crawled to the roof's edge and peered over, they discovered the guards had gone. The alley was at least temporarily empty. Apparently the guards were either over at the side of the building, waiting for them to come back down that way, or they'd disappeared into the night to avoid confronting the police.

"Now what?"

Tarik nodded to the fire escape below them. "I'll lower you to the platform. Hurry."

"What about you?"

"Right behind you, love. Go now."

Jass nodded and swung herself off the edge. God, she was spectacular.

Tarik leaned down and went flat on his stomach, grabbing hold of her forearms as she clung to the edge. The second his grip was sure, Jass took her fingers off the edge, and he eased her down into the darkness.

"Good enough," she whispered.

He hoped to hell she was right, and then he let her go. In another instant a clang and then a thump told him her feet had hit the metal fire escape.

Mumbling a curse under his breath for whoever had put him in the position of dangling over a dark abyss again, Tarik lowered himself over the roof edge and prayed he was lined up with the fire escape platform. After a big cleansing breath of air, he opened his hands and let go, dropping into yet another endless, starfilled night.

* * *

Jass managed to pull Tarik into her arms to keep him from falling into the street below as he'd dropped off the roof feet first. Out of breath and a little bruised from both her own fall and from being a cushion for his, she was grateful that they were both still alive.

But Tarik didn't give her the time to take a break or give thanks.

"Let's go." He shoved her down the fire-escape stairs ahead of him. "Keep moving. Those cops are pulling up in front now."

She scrambled down the one flight and planted her feet on the pavement. "Back to the car?"

"Yeah. But stick to the alleyways if you can. Stay in the shadows."

Earlier today Jass had memorized the streets around the samba club. Heading off now, she wished for a pair of running shoes instead of these silly heeled boots. The boots had been okay for use on the roof, but running full out in the dark on crumbling city sidewalks would've been a heck of a lot easier in a good pair of Nikes.

Tarik stayed a step behind, though she figured he could easily outdistance her if he wanted to. He was moving like a cheetah. Smooth and sleek and precise. On the other hand, she was plenty fast too as her heart pumped double-time with adrenaline. In fight-or-flight mode, she ran almost a half mile out of their way, winding through the alleys and down half-deserted streets. Still, in fifteen minutes they were nearing the car.

"Hold on a minute." Tarik stopped and jogged in place. "Isn't this where we left the headpieces to our costumes?"

Gulping in air, she wondered how he could sound this cool. She was nearly out of breath and his breathing was barely labored.

"Yes." She pointed at the rain barrel down the block.

"We can't leave them for the cops to find." He raced ahead and started pulling out feathered hats and a swashbuckler's sword.

Exactly what she didn't need—more stuff to weigh her down. But she took the monumental headgear under her arm when he handed it to her and started down the street toward their car once again.

The sound of sirens getting closer rang through the quiet, putting the hair up on the back of her neck. Then it hit her. Why did the streets seem deserted? It hadn't been quiet when they'd first come this way.

As they reached their car, she gritted out, "Where the heck is everyone? Might as well be carrying a painted sign announcing our guilt."

Tarik didn't answer but raced to the passenger door, jerked it open and jumped in. He slammed the door behind him as she managed to crawl in behind the wheel, squished her costume down at her feet and fastened her seat belt.

"Here come the good guys," Tarik said as he gave a quick glance up ahead at the flashing lights. "Move."

Jass jammed the car in gear, grabbed the wheel with both hands and did a quick one-eighty in the middle of the street. She had to get off the main road. But which way to go?

Taking three quick turns in succession, she blindly roared down alleyways and doubled back over the same streets where they'd been running. But she didn't seem to be losing the cops. There simply wasn't any way to hide without any other traffic around. Flashing lights and screaming sirens stayed right behind them.

"Take the next left," Tarik commanded.

She turned without question, sliding hard on two wheels. And drove right into the tail end of the traffic jam to end all traffic jams. Bumper-to-bumper cars lined the street and blocked the way.

"Brilliant, Einstein. Now what do you suggest?"

"Quick, change places with me. I'll drive."

"Drive where?" She gestured to the line of cars practically parked on top of each other in the street ahead.

"Just go. But don't get out of the car."

With a quick glance behind them and an exasperated sigh, she figured she had no choice. "Right."

"Thank you."

He'd better sound appropriately grateful. And this had better work to get them off the hook. She would hate facing the Rio police without any idea of who'd tipped them off or how they'd been turned in. No telling if someone had paid to get them out of the way—or if a few of those cops wouldn't be a little trigger-happy.

No, she decided firmly as she undid her seat belt and started over the console. They couldn't face the authorities. They needed to find a way out. If not by outracing the cops, then by hiding from them.

"What's with the traffic jam?" she muttered as he slid his body in under hers.

Instead of answering, Tarik sucked in a breath and stilled. Yeah, she'd felt it too as the curve of her bottom brushed over his crotch. All of a sudden she was the woman on top. And he was the utterly masculine male on the bottom.

Bad timing. She sucked in her own breath. Extremely bad timing.

Fortunately, she was a pro. "Excuse me. Uh, can you keep going, please?" She laid a hand on his shoulder to help lift her weight off of him.

But that didn't do much to help. The heat from his body seared her hand and sent an earthquake rumbling back up her arm and into her belly.

"If you'll scoot a little farther—"

"Uff." She threw her body into the seat he'd vacated.

Tarik maneuvered himself into the driver's seat and locked down his seat belt. "The traffic jam is all about the parade. See the pedestrians crowding the sidewalks trying to get a better view? Nothing's moving until the parade goes past." He gave her a quick once-over. "Hang on."

Throwing the car's transmission into low, he nosed the front bumper toward the sidewalk to their left and inched ahead into the crowd.

"Stop! Are you nuts? You'll kill—"

She stopped talking and held her breath as pedestrians scattered. The sidewalks here had no curbs and this one wasn't quite as wide as the car.

She flicked a glance behind them and saw two cars pulling into the space at the end of the line that they'd left. The police—or someone impersonating them—jumped out and came in their direction.

Tarik kept the car steadily moving forward. Faster and faster, heedless of the human beings in his way. By now paradegoers were beginning to complain as they were unceremoniously shoved aside by a car. Shouts erupted as holes opened in front of their car's bumper and then promptly closed in behind them when they drove through. Suddenly they were completely surrounded by irate costumed paradegoers and the police were nowhere in sight.

Everyone was shouting and raising their fists. Jass wasn't thrilled about putting these people out, nearly killing them and taking the chance of a riot. But she was relieved the cops had been left behind in the process.

"Don't breathe easy yet. Those cops are now on foot. As slow as we have to go in the crowd, they'll catch up too soon. I think we should bail. We'll stand a much better shot on foot."

Jass nodded and undid her seat belt.

"Put on your hat," Tarik ordered as he turned the car off and eased open the door. "We'll blend in."

He was right. She bent to adjust her hat while Tarik jumped out from the driver's side door. By the time she turned to open her own door, an angry mob was outside the window.

Trying to open her door, she muttered, "Hey, sorry. Can't you take a joke? Isn't this a party?"

She shoved hard against the mass of humanity pushing against the car door on the other side. But the more she put her shoulder into it, the more difficult it became to move the door even an inch. She would never get out of the car before the cops arrived at this rate.

Right then the car began to rock from side to side. Jass had visions of being caught in the front seat as the crowds turned the sedan over and set it ablaze.

She grit her teeth and worked even harder

to get the door open. Nothing she did would budge it.

But all of a sudden the door flew open and her body was pulled free. But how? Before she could react, she felt herself being dragged through the crowds. The police? Was she on her way to jail?

"Keep moving." No, when she looked up, it was Tarik.

She should have known.

He was propelling them through the throng faster than she would've thought possible. She chanced a glance behind them. Only a few yards from the car and it had already disappeared inside the mass of humanity.

Tarik threw his arm around her shoulders and jerked her closer to his chest. It was a protective motion that should've annoyed her with its macho implications. Instead, she was grateful for the cover.

The music and the noisy revelry grew to

thunderous proportions. Yet they kept shoving their way forward through the crowds.

"You still with me?" Tarik hesitated only a second.

"Go," she screamed over the din.

He pushed them out into an opening in the humanity. And suddenly they were smack in the middle of the street—right in the midst of the samba dancers as they paraded along the boulevard doing their show.

But it was open enough here in the street to actually run. Tarik almost lifted her entirely off her feet as he dashed from side to side, dodging dancers and drummers alike.

Jass expected another riot. But this time they only received a few shouts and lots of laughter and good-natured applause. Several blocks down the way Tarik stopped long enough to take a bow along with the dancers.

"Quit being a ham," she gritted out. "Get me out of here."

He laughed and dragged them off the street

on the other side and back into the crowds. "We wouldn't have gotten that far without the costumes. Thought we'd be clever and use them to the fullest."

Jass tsked at him. "Now how do we get back to the hotel?"

"Are those boots made for walking?"

"How far is it?"

"Only a couple of miles. Mostly downhill. It'll be a good chance for us to get to know each other."

Shaking her head and trying to keep the smile off her face, Jass pulled the heavy headpiece off. "My boots are perfectly fine for walking, thank you. In fact, you'd best keep up the pace or I'll leave you in my dust, Kadir."

With that, she turned in a circle, looking for a familiar landmark or street sign.

"Lost?" Tarik took her by the hand and hustled down the street. "Come on. Maybe we'll be better off with my slower pace. But whatever we do, let's move it now."

Chapter 8

Tarik kept hold of her hand, more to settle his own nerves than for any other reason. Jass tried halfheartedly to break away. But when he refused to let her loose, she relaxed and remained comfortably beside him, keeping up with the pace he set.

"We can't run or we'll call attention to our movements," he told her. "If we stroll, we'll look like any other tourists or paradegoers. Good enough?"

"I suppose."

She sounded so petulant that he nearly laughed. Instead, he decided to give her an out and let her go back to being her sarcastic self.

"Don't I get a thank-you for saving your ass back there? My driving skills saved the day."

Narrowing her lips to tiny white lines, she simply stared at him. The quiet was unlike her and he couldn't let it be.

"Okay, maybe it was a little over-the-top for me to head right into a crowd of innocent by-standers, but it did the trick, didn't it?"

She shrugged—a totally uncharacteristic movement. That clinched it for him. He had to find a way to get her talking again.

He took a quick look around at the many other costumed pedestrians strolling along the sidewalks and heading toward the beach side of town like they were. Cars streamed by, going to different neighborhoods or possibly heading toward the parade in the other direction. No one paid them any attention. A pirate and the cat woman easily blended right into the revelry of the night.

"I sure wish I knew who set us up tonight." He kept his voice down, but he wasn't worried about being overheard. "You have any ideas on that subject?"

"Not really. The only people who could've been aware we'd be at Eltsin's tonight were the local CIA operatives and the Task Force. I'll have Ed get to the bottom of it while we stay on the job."

Now there was a subject he would bet she'd warm up to. "Speaking of Ed, he seems inordinately cautious about your welfare. Like you're more than simply a superior and his employee. You two have some sort of history?"

She gave him a wary glance before apparently deciding he had no ulterior motive for asking. "We go way back. Ed and my father were partners on covert missions for the Agency for many years. I first met Ed when I was a little girl, right after my mother died."

"I understand your father was killed while on an operation for the CIA."

She nodded quietly before clearing her throat. "Yes. I was in my first year of college at the time. Dad and I had a huge fight right before he left for the mission." She breathed in and out. "I never got to tell him I was sorry."

"What was the fight about?" Okay, that was too personal a question for brand-new partners, but he didn't care. He wanted to know more about her.

Jass didn't seem to mind his prying. In fact, she seemed quite willing to talk.

"I was switching my major at the time. I'd been in pre-law because that's what Dad wanted. But I wanted the more hands-on approach of law enforcement. He expected a lawyer in the family. I wanted to be a covert agent like he was."

"What degree did you end up with?"

"I almost quit altogether after Dad died." She sighed and he knew she was thinking back to those terrible days when she'd first become an orphan. "If it hadn't been for Ed stepping in and offering to help me get a job with the Agency after graduation and giving me a little financial assistance, I might have ended up as a waitress or a security guard."

She screwed up her mouth and shook her head. "I graduated pre-law, in Dad's memory. But I went to work for the CIA immediately after getting my degree. Ed made all the difference. He coached me and cajoled me into graduating and then took me under his wing at the Agency." Raw emotion filled her voice. "I owe him my career. And…more. I owe him for his friendship when I needed it the most."

"Did your father ever say why he didn't want his daughter following in his footsteps?"

She took another big breath. "Not that I can

remember. He always said the job made a person hard. And too indifferent about human life."

"From where I sit, it hasn't seemed to make you hard," Tarik said with a softness in his tone that surprised even him. "You were sincerely concerned for the people in that crowd of pedestrians back there."

Instead of a smile, Jass scowled. "Right. Remind me that I'm not as tough as you are. Rub it in. I deserve it."

"What? No, I didn't mean it that way. You're plenty tough when you need to be. It's just... you're also tender—which is a good thing in my book."

"Humph." Jass lifted her chin and strode ahead with more purpose.

Tarik squeezed her hand and she slowed enough to come back to his side. "You remind me a little of my mother," he told her, more for something to say than to share something about himself.

"I thought your mother died when you were young."

"I was five." He did not want to have this conversation. Thoughts of his mother always made his chest ache with the memories.

"Why do I remind you of her?"

Okay, he'd asked for this. "Her family comes from a nomadic Bedouin background, same as my father's. But unlike the Kadirs, her family is still living in the deserts today and surviving on simple trade the way they have for centuries. They exist right on the edge of civilization, only slightly shy of savagery.

"Until my grandfather passed away a few years ago," Tarik continued. "He swore by the old ways. His sons had to be warriors and his daughters had to be tough enough to survive under the harshest of conditions."

Tarik wished he could find a way out of this,

but he knew he would have to at least be sincere with Jass—and more truthful than he'd allowed himself to be since he was a devastated five-year-old. Talking about his dead mother in intimate detail hurt.

Sighing quietly, he said the words he'd long avoided even thinking about. "My mother was raised to be tough, but she was also a princess of the tribe. Her grandmother insisted she be sent away to college, where she met and married my father." He caught her gaze. "If you'd been introduced to her, you would never have known about her upbringing. She was sophisticated and genteel. A lady in every sense of the word. And she loved her sons with a quiet ferociousness I've never seen since."

But he had a feeling Jass would love with the same kind of passionate intensity. For some crazy reason the idea made him suddenly long to be the object of all that fiery passion.

He shook off the unwelcome vulnerability.

His mission could mean uncovering a threat to the entire world, and as such it was not the time or place for personal introspection and need. Maybe he should try sneaking out and getting himself laid later—in order to release the tension. In his wayward youth, a little flash-bang of a sexual nature would've taken the edge off long enough for him to finish an assignment and put his mind back in the game.

But he'd matured a lot in the last couple of years. Quick tumbles with complete strangers no longer held any appeal. He wasn't looking for any kind of commitment either—his family's covert war prevented thoughts of long-term romance. And even though both his brothers had found women to die for, he couldn't imagine bringing someone he loved into the middle of this much danger.

Still, a woman would have to mean something to him now before he fell into bed. Something more than a way to release a little tension—despite what he'd said to Jass yesterday when he'd been trying to tease her into becoming more comfortable playacting as his girlfriend.

Though at the time, when he'd said the two of them needed to have a good old-fashioned roll in the hay, he had meant every word. In fact, it still sounded like a good idea. More than good. It sounded like paradise.

But he couldn't help wondering why the conflict between what he thought he believed and what his body craved seemed wildly at odds when it came to Jass.

Compassion glistened in her eyes. "Your mother sounds like a special woman. I wish I could've known her."

"You two would've had a lot in common. You're a lot like she was. Tough when you need to be. And tender underneath."

Maybe that was it. Maybe Jass's personality felt as familiar and comfortable as cozy memories of the only woman who'd ever loved him. And therefore she must already mean something important to him and wouldn't be merely an anonymous roll in the hay. But he sure wished he could figure out exactly why that had happened so fast.

As they stepped off the elevator down the hall from their hotel room, Jass felt somebody watching. She took Tarik's arm and sidled up close to him before casually checking both ends of the hallway. She couldn't spot anyone when she looked, but someone was there nonetheless.

As they neared their hotel-room door, the elevator doors opened again and when they turned back, a waiter stepped off carrying a tray. He came in their direction but as he came closer, she saw it was Station Chief Bosque in disguise.

Jass jumped in and went with their cover story. "Ohh, is that for us?" She managed a broad smile and turned to Tarik. "Zohdi, darling, did you order a late dinner as a surprise? How thoughtful of you. I'm famished."

Tarik didn't answer but used his card key to open the door and then turned to the supposed waiter. "Bring it inside."

As Bosque brushed past Tarik, he spoke under his breath. "You've had visitors. Inside long enough to plant bugs. Stay in character, but meet me on the terrace."

Once they were inside, Bosque began setting up the dining table for two. He laid out candles, a late supper and even a bottle of chilled wine.

Her brain raced with ways to get them out on the terrace without being too obvious. She waltzed over to Tarik, went up on tiptoes and planted a kiss against his lips. She'd wanted quick and flirty. Instead, the heat and the chemistry between them flared up and nearly knocked her down.

She pulled away, but lingered long enough

to lick his lips and then her own. "It's awfully warm in here, isn't it?"

Tarik look slightly stunned, but he ran with her lead. "Very much so, my love. And it's such a nice night." He shrugged out of his pirate's hat and jacket and headed toward the terrace doors. "Let's get some air."

He threw open the glass doors and stepped through to the wide terrace.

"Wait for me." She started out behind him. "What a wonderful view. Too bad we can't have supper out here."

Bosque lifted his head and spoke while she stepped outside. "I'm sorry, madam. There is not enough room on the terrace for the setting. However—" He picked up the wine and two glasses. "You may enjoy your wine before supper outside if you prefer. If you'll allow me to pour?"

He followed both of them out through the French doors and then quietly closed them behind him. "Did you two run into trouble tonight? We found your car abandoned." He poured Tarik a full glass and handed it over. "We've received word that our man inside Eltsin's operation was killed earlier. What do you know about it?"

Tarik set the glass down on the ledge overlooking the bay. "We found the body. But somebody was trying to set us up. We barely got out before the cops arrived."

Bosque cursed under his breath. "I was afraid of that. I've already started an internal investigation, but it'll take time. Do you want to call off the mission?"

"Not a chance." Jass threw a glance toward Tarik and he nodded his agreement. "It's possible Eltsin was only fishing. Checking to see who showed up at his place. I don't believe he knows for sure it was us or he'd have sent goons to take us out, not to spy on us."

"Agreed," Tarik put in. "This mission is too

important to abort. Escalating danger is all part of the job."

"All right, if you're sure then." Bosque handed Jass a glass of sparkling wine. "We'd better leave the bugs in place. We don't want Eltsin's crowd to know we're on to their game. I'm guessing they set up cameras or listening devices in the sitting room and maybe even in the bedroom." He nodded once. "Assume that's where they are for now. I'll double-check the bath and the bedroom terrace for bugs before I leave. Keep the act on everywhere but there."

Oh hell. Jass hadn't thought of that. *The act.* She and Tarik would have to continue pretending to be lovers even while alone. All night.

It was a good thing she believed in what Tarik had told Bosque. The mission was too important to back out of their cover story now.

But later on her resolve might prove easier said than done. Starting to sweat in the sultry sea air, she took a sip of cool wine and let it slide down her suddenly dry throat. The mission was about to become particularly difficult. A long night of sharing a single bed in front of a camera with one of the sexiest men she'd ever met might be her toughest assignment yet.

But she had to keep in mind that Tarik was not Zohdi. Tarik was out of bounds. A partner. A buddy. Not a lover. And on top of that, he was still the man her handler swore was someone she should be wary about trusting.

Ed's opinion didn't seem as much of a problem now that she and Tarik had completed one night's mission. But if she didn't watch out, Tarik could easily become too important in her life. She couldn't have that. It would interfere with her self-image as a serious, dedicated professional.

As much as he had saved their lives and she was beginning to rely on him as a competent partner, in her mind, Tarik was still kind of a clown. A gorgeous, sexy charmer who could become anything as long as it was in his own self-interest. The exact opposite of the man she'd always assumed would capture her heart. A man like her father.

Reciting once again the mantra she'd decided to live by, Jass reminded herself that despite her intense reactions toward Tarik Kadir, it was only her hormones talking. She could handle him. She could handle anything that came her way. After all, she was a pro.

Tarik tried to pretend the heat and the obvious lust between them were not serious concerns. But he knew better.

When the woman wanted to prove she could masquerade being in love, she did it in spades. His still slamming pulse did not bode well for the cover story tonight. Cool. He needed to remain cool.

A man like Zohdi did not lose his mind over a few kisses. Yet it was all Tarik could do a few minutes ago not to fall down on his knees and beg her to kiss him again.

What would he be like later? In bed with the cameras running? Could he restrain his own raging lust and yet fake making love to her? This whole business was definitely not what he'd signed up for.

Bosque feigned giving them turndown service as he checked the bathroom and bedroom terrace for bugs. But he was ready to leave them alone much too soon to suit Tarik.

On his way out, Bosque murmured in his ear, "Bath and terrace are clear. Found a hidden camera in a wall sconce in the bedroom. Good luck."

Yeah, right.

Filling his lungs with what he hoped was fortifying air, Tarik returned to Jass's side. "Let's share this meal, my sweet, and proceed to the dessert." Taking on Zohdi's persona again, he kissed her hand. "We're overdue for time alone."

He caught the quick but frantic look of panic in Jass's eyes, but when she spoke, she was all Celile. "Hmmm. I can't wait."

After they'd picked at their food for an hour and found inane subjects to discuss while sitting across the table casting lustful gazes at each other, it was time for them to play their parts as two lovers alone. He stood and pulled her into his arms, making a big show for the camera.

"Enough of this." He looked down into her eyes. "Come to bed with me."

Her gaze carried not a trace of panic this time. In fact, Jass seemed the perfect picture of a woman so much in love she would do anything her man asked. He was the one worrying about the act.

She stepped back and looked up at him

through long, thick lashes. "Help me out of this costume, darling."

Ah, hell. He scooped her up in his arms and strode into the bedroom, slamming the door to the sitting room behind him. He would deal with the one camera in the bedroom because he knew where it was located.

Positioning himself between the wall sconce and the bed, he let Jass slide down his body until her feet hit the floor. "The only camera in here is on the wall behind me," he whispered as he helped her regain her footing. "Stay where they can't see you."

She didn't act as if she understood him, but he noticed her give the wall behind him a quick glance over his shoulder. Then twisting around, she presented him with her back.

"The zipper, love. I can't reach."

Swallowing hard, Tarik reached for her zipper but his fingers froze mid-motion. He didn't want to expose her to prying eyes this way.

Was stripping her in public supposed to be part of his job description?

He made a quick decision. "My costume first, sweetheart. I want to take my time with yours."

If anyone was going to be the star of this strip show, it would be him. His naked body would be the thing they had to focus on first. And he hoped to hell they got an eyeful through that camera lens.

Pulling the pirate's shirt and undershirt over his head, he pitched them behind him without looking. With any luck they would land on the wall sconce, but thus far his luck hadn't been running hot.

Next he quickly dispensed with the pirate's boots and pants. Standing there stark naked was no big deal for him. He could care less who saw what. But once again he faced the problem of helping Jass with her zipper. Her back was still turned and he felt grateful for small favors.

Could he maneuver them under the bedcovers

before she must face both him and the camera full on?

Moving in close behind her back, he wrapped an arm around her shoulders and began lowering the zipper with the other. The process seemed to take forever. His body grew harder with every millimeter.

Without clearly thinking about what he was doing and where they were, he buried his nose in her neck and breathed in the lush scent of her. Every cell, every atom in his body went on full alert and rebelled at the sudden onslaught of intoxicating need. He desired the woman under the wig and brown contact lenses. But that's not who he held.

She tugged at his arms and he let loose long enough for her to wiggle out of the cat suit. Standing there in only a red bra and thong panties, she still had her back turned. She hadn't allowed herself to be observed in anything more than what she might've worn to the beach. *Good work, partner.*

What would Zohdi do at this point?

Same thing Tarik would do if all else were equal. Groaning, he reached down and swept her up in his arms again. Without turning them around, he carried her to the bed and unceremoniously dumped her there, jumping in after her a split second later.

He threw himself over her, covering her body with his own. Holding her still, he placed both hands on the sides of her head as he insinuated himself between her thighs.

Closing in for a kiss, he whispered against her lips, "I'll cover us with the blanket in a moment. Just play along for now."

But then Jass moaned. Not out of any pain or act, but she seemed clearly lost in a real passion. Apparently she wasn't playing the same game he was.

She squirmed and opened her eyes to look up

at him with a glazed look. Her expression was enough of a shock to make him forget all about his mission. All about the camera. Until finally, he even forgot his own name.

Chapter 9

What is Tarik saying?

Jass struggled to come out of her haze and listen, but the blood boiled in her ears. With her pulse screaming through her veins as though she were pulling down five Gs, her body throbbed with passion. And all because of the masculine body currently lying suggestively between her legs.

Geez. She bit the inside of her cheek hard enough to snap herself out of it. They were supposedly working a sting. She was Celile. But he was not the real Zohdi.

Work. Work. Work. This was an important assignment and not the most intimate experience she'd ever had. Worse even than the idea of taking a risk with her career, there'd been a camera trained on them this whole time.

She'd lost her mind. But, oh man, what a terrific way to go insane. The sexual chemistry between the two of them left her soaring. Tarik's mere touch jolted her with an intense excitement, sparking a conflagration that had sent her up in flames. His naked and aroused body surprised her, but it shouldn't have. He was so much more than she imagined. The most potent male she'd ever seen.

Like spontaneous combustion, she'd found herself wet and set to explode.

But they were only acting for their mission. Right?

Remember the mission.

"Hold on." Tarik left her long enough to drag the covers up and over their heads, covering them completely from view.

How could he remain unaffected? Well, not totally unaffected, she'd noticed. He was hot and pulsing…and huge. He'd been ready just like she was.

But his mind had stayed in the game. A trait she'd better learn how to mimic.

"Laugh," he demanded in a raspy whisper. "Or giggle. Anything that makes it seem as though we're doing what it looks like in this bed."

His words actually made some sense through her clearing fog. At last. She wiggled out from underneath his body and rolled over to face him—while both of them remained hidden under the covers.

Watching him closely, she opened her mouth and let out one of the loudest moans imaginable. "Ah. Ah. Ah." She forced the volume higher. "Oh, Zohdi. Oh. Oh."

Finally, she wound herself up and screamed incoherently. A thing she had never done during the throes of passion in her entire lifetime.

Tarik actually smiled as he murmured low, "Nice work, agent. I'd like a repeat performance someday. But not for the cameras."

That did it. He had to move away. Now.

"Get out of bed and turn off the lights, Zohdi." She gritted her teeth. "And then bring me a robe."

Why hadn't the man thought to turn out the lights in the first place?

In a hushed tone, Tarik answered. "Okay, but I'm betting turning off the lights won't help. The camera is probably NVC, night-vision capable. Most surveillance equipment is set up that way. I'll gladly get the robes." He scowled and rolled out from under the blankets, leaving her covered and furious.

Seconds later he pulled down the covers and immediately threw one of the terry bathrobes over her. "Get up, Celile," he announced in a loud voice. "You need a shower and I have work to do on the laptop."

"What did you say?" It was easy to fake a little indignation. She felt every bit of Celile's part.

Tarik turned his back. "Get up."

"Well, isn't that romantic? You bastard." She shoved her arms into the robe and stood. "I'm going. But if you think for one minute that you're in for a repeat performance tonight, you are out of your mind. You and your damned laptop can sleep out on the terrace."

Grasping the robe around her like a shield, Jass marched into the bathroom and slammed the door. Once alone and out of camera range, she leaned both hands heavily on the countertop. Hanging her head and breathing in and out through her mouth, she tried to calm her shaky nerves.

Realization began to sink in. He had actually picked a fight in order to save them from having to sleep together tonight. The whole scene back there suddenly became clear. Everything he'd done in the bedroom—stripping himself and not her, carrying her to the bed and covering them from view—all of it was done for her benefit. To save her from embarrassment.

Tarik Kadir had honor. He'd wanted her as much as she'd wanted him, but he wasn't going to give in to it in front of an audience. Amazing.

She tore off the Celile wig and popped out the brown-colored contacts, ready to scrub off all traces of the bitch who was currently ruling her life. A hot shower was definitely in order.

But then again, maybe Jass would be a lot better off taking a cold shower. The more she thought about Tarik in the buff, the more she wished he hadn't been quite as professional and thoughtful. She was starting to believe that he'd been right and they would indeed have a repeat performance someday.

But at that time he would *not* be dressed in sheik's clothing and she would *not* be wearing a brown wig and brown contact lens or answering to the name Celile. And there would definitely not be any cameras allowed.

It might've been one of the longest nights of his life. Grumpy and stiff, Tarik sat across the breakfast table from Jass, drinking coffee and feeling miserable about ever opening his big mouth last night. If he had only shut up, stayed in bed and not deliberately picked that fight with her, it could have turned into one of the best nights he'd ever had.

The only thing saving him from abject misery this morning was Jass's expression. She still resembled Celile, but there was something about the way she looked at him that told a different story. When she'd apologized for the argument that had kept him out on the terrace all night, she'd used Celile's voice. But the emotion in her eyes said his real partner was every bit as sorry for their difficult circumstances.

He reached over and took her hand, also feeling a little sorry that he still couldn't speak from the heart. "You are forgiven, my darling Celile. And I apologize for being an ass. Let's spend the day making it up to each other."

Jass opened her mouth, but right then a loud knock on the suite door captured their attention.

"I'll get it." She stood and went toward the door.

He watched her move, fascinated by the sure and steady stride. And by the curve of her hips. The way she filled out her blouse. And by the ever-so-slight pout she always wore on her lips.

God help him, but he was becoming helpless to think of anything else when he was around his partner.

Before Jass could make sure it was Bosque, the door burst open and a couple of well-dressed goons barged into the room as if they'd had their own key. They both pulled snub-nosed Uzis from under their suit coats and pointed them at Jass.

"You will come with us." The more heavyset one of the duo spoke in Russian.

Tarik was on his feet in an instant and moving toward Jass before he even realized what he was doing.

She didn't seem fazed. "Put those weapons away, you imbeciles." She made the demand in the best Russian dialect he'd ever heard.

Tarik froze where he stood. She was handling it far better without him.

The man with the gun suddenly looked as if someone had punched him in the gut. He shook his head as though he were a prize fighter who'd heard bells ringing.

"But the boss…he requests your presence for *Carnivale* this weekend." The other man's hand began to shake as he slid the Uzi back under his jacket.

"Mr. Eltsin will not be happy to learn you treated his guests and customers in such a manner." Jass threw her hands on her hips in a perfect imitation of something Celile would do. "We'll accompany you to Mr. Eltsin's. But we will only leave after finishing our breakfast and packing an overnight bag."

She turned her back on the men as though she could care less about their weapons. "Wait out in the hall."

Tarik fought to keep the grin off his face. Man, she was spectacular. He followed her into the deep, walk-in closet in the bedroom and found her shoving high-tech gear into a collapsible backpack.

"Aren't you going to need some clothes, too?"

She glanced up at him and scowled. "A couple of sexy outfits and a few cosmetics, maybe. But this equipment is much more important. You pack the weapons."

"Okay, boss lady." With a silent chuckle, he went to work.

All the passion and romance, even the friendship, was buried for now. The covert agents were back on the job.

They rode through the streets of Rio in the backseat of a silver Mercedes sedan. Tarik's gut instincts were shouting that this was the wrong move for them to make. He didn't believe starting out with two well-armed goons, without first having contact with either the Task Force or his brothers, could lead to anything good.

As their sedan climbed into the hills above the city and drove past the shantytown areas known as favelas, his bigger worry became how to control Jass. Since Eltsin's henchmen had shown up, she'd become Celile in a deeper way than ever before. He could no longer find

Jass inside her eyes. But even with his unease, he still trusted her to do whatever necessary for the mission. She was a professional and his partner.

All along the scenic drive at the crest of the mountains, Tarik stared out his window at the city and the bay spreading below them. Tiny white sailboats floated on the turquoise blue of Guanabara Bay. Sparkling white sands blistered in the hot sun of Ipanema Beach. The greens and grays of Sugarloaf Mountain in the distance were silhouetted like a picture postcard against puffy lavender and pink clouds.

Everything seemed painted in Technicolor.

His senses tended to remain on full alert during any mission. But for some reason today, on this mission, the world was brighter, sweeter than ever before.

The big hitch in the perfection, of course, was knowing Jass could be stepping into a rat's nest of trouble at Eltsin's place, completely unprepared for what Tarik felt was coming. Yes, she'd fallen deeper into her cover and had become Celile, the Messenger. But Tarik knew the Taj would be there. And they were trouble with a capital T everywhere they went.

Worse yet, he would have to avoid being around the Taj as much as possible. Since he was disguised at Sheik Zohdi, Tarik didn't imagine the Taj Zabbar officials would immediately recognize him as a Kadir. But he would have to be particularly careful with his accent, and under no circumstance could he let on that he understood their language.

One slipup would mean disaster for the Kadirs, for this mission and for Jass. That meant he was left dealing with the fact that she would have to be the public face of their mission. Tarik took a breath, wishing he could talk to her privately.

After another half hour of silence, Andrei Eltsin's gated villa appeared like a castle in the lush green mountainside overlooking the sprawling Rio metropolis and picturesque ocean far below. Tarik steeled himself to arrive in the manner of the mysterious terrorist he'd been playing. Rearranging his head scarf to partially block his face, he reviewed his game plan. Covert work was all about showmanship. And becoming a dangerous and volatile Middle Eastern terrorist meant shutting his mouth and keeping to himself. Despite the circumstances and the danger to Jass.

The Mercedes passed through a heavily guarded gate and rolled up the long drive past multicolored flowers, evergreen shrubs and a manicured green lawn. They pulled up in front of a sprawling and opulent Moroccan-style building and stopped before twenty-foot-tall, mahogany doors. It was one hell of a dramatic entryway with ornate grillwork and terra-cotta tiles on the steps. Yes, indeed, this Eltsin character had a penchant for high drama.

The two goons bailed out of the car as soon as it came to a stop and opened the back passenger doors. "The boss wants you to relinquish your weapons before you enter his private quarters. Turn them over to us now and avoid being frisked inside."

Jass came out of the Mercedes like a queen. "Not a chance, big boy." She held on to her wide-brimmed straw hat with one hand and put the other on the goon's chest. "Now do I look like I have any weapons on me?"

The Russian's face colored with embarrassment as his eyes raked down her tight-fitting zebra-print dress, long legs and strappy sandals. "No, ma'am. But it's my job."

She waved him off. "Nonsense. And as for Sheik Zohdi, I would not advise anyone to try taking his weapons. Not if you wish to live to see tomorrow."

Tarik took that as his cue, eased out of the

backseat and stretched his legs. The goon by his door backed up out of his way.

Jass moved a step closer to the villa's front door, speaking over her shoulder as though she must be obeyed without question. "Take us to see Mr. Eltsin immediately. He will straighten all of this out. I'm sure he does not want to offend one of his best customers." She sighed devisively. "Oh, and you boys better bring the bags inside."

Yeah, the lady was good.

Inside the house, Tarik had some trouble keeping his mouth from gaping open. Talk about ostentatious wealth. Crystal chandeliers, which looked as if they belonged in a palace rather than in a villa, hung from forty-foot ceilings. Hand woven Persian carpets adorned the travertine tile floors. A hand-carved, exotic wood staircase soared up three flights in the grand entrance hall.

Everywhere he looked was gold leaf. Gold

on the woodwork. Golden goblets and golden threads in plush fabrics.

The Kadir family had done well in their businesses over the years. But Tarik couldn't remember ever seeing wealth on crude display this way. Business must be better than good for the suppliers of weapons of mass destruction these days.

"The boss is waiting." One of the goons pointed his weapon toward a sunken living room off to the left.

Jass spun and strode down the few steps as if she owned the place. "Mr. Eltsin," she said in Russian. "How nice of you to invite us to spend a few days with you. This is such a lovely villa."

Eltsin stood alone by a bar, with a cocktail glass full of either vodka or tequila in his hand. "I'm pleased you could join me, Ms. Kocak." He'd spoken in lightly accented English and made it clear that he would prefer carrying on in that language.

Once again Tarik became wary. Did the Russian have some idea that his guests were fluent English speakers and not who they claimed to be?

Fortunately for Tarik, Sheik Zohdi was more conversant in English than he was in Russian. Perhaps Eltsin had investigated and found that out.

As if the man was answering his unspoken questions, Eltsin said, "Thank you for coming, Sheik Zohdi. My humble home is open to you. We will speak in English this weekend to make my guests comfortable. Not all of them are as at ease with Russian as you are, Ms. Kocak."

Tarik believed the Taj Zabbar would be in attendance since he'd overheard them talking about coming. Would anyone else be there? Of course, knowing the Taj as he did, they would probably refuse to speak in Russian even though he was positive they understood it perfectly well.

"It does not matter," Jass told him offhandedly. She'd made sure to heavily accent her English.

"Good. Now, before I offer you my hospitality, I would prefer it if you'd disarm yourselves."

Jass opened her mouth to make a response, but Eltsin held up his hand and interrupted. "I had sincerely hoped you would voluntarily give up your weapons while in my home. But I'll have them taken from you if that's your choice."

Tarik didn't want Jass to endure either a search or an argument. Stepping closer to Eltsin, he carefully withdrew the Walther from his jacket pocket.

"I will voluntarily give mine up." He hesitated with his fingers on the butt end of the gun. "To my knowledge, Ms. Kocak is unarmed, but no one touches her. Understood? In addition,

I expect your word on our safety while we remain under your roof."

Eltsin ignored him and nodded to one of his henchman, standing in the doorway. The man gingerly approached Tarik and put his hand out for the gun.

"Your word, Eltsin?"

"Of course. But Ms. Kocak…"

Jass moved closer to Eltsin, nearly rubbing up against the Russian. "I carry a small weapon in my briefcase. It is for self-defense only. And it is tiny, really. Nearly useless."

"No weapons in my home."

"Certainly," Jass said dismissively. "As you wish. We are all civilized here."

She reached into her bag and turned over the smaller-sized Ruger she'd stashed there. Tarik handed over his weapon to the henchman at the same time.

"When do we get to meet our competitors, Mr. Eltsin?" Jass moved closer to Tarik and farther away from Eltsin. A telling move that Eltsin clearly understood.

After the tension surrounding the weapon transfer, Eltsin suddenly looked at ease. "Do not think of this weekend as only business, Ms. Kocak." His mouth actually turned up in a strange version of a smile. "I want you two to enjoy yourselves. I think you'll find the pool and gardens are quite delightful. Please take advantage of them with my compliments."

Jass lowered her shoulders and smiled back warmly. "Why thank you. We'll do that."

Tarik wanted to make a couple of things clear first. "I am not much on leisure time, Mr. Eltsin." He used the low, threatening voice of the sheik to make his point. "I expect the privacy to conduct my business and to spend time alone with Ms. Kocak."

He put his hand possessively on Jass's shoulder. "And, I expect that our personal business papers and computers will be protected from prying eyes."

"There is a safe in your room," Eltsin said without any trace of rancor. "And I give you my word neither you nor your things will be bothered while you're at my home. But I sincerely hope you and Ms. Kocak will spend at least a little time relaxing while you are here. All work and no play, you know."

An American cliché? Eltsin must be suspicious.

"All work and no play—what could that mean, Mr. Eltsin?" Jass had caught the odd remark and with a glance at Eltsin, casually wound her arm through Tarik's.

Eltsin smiled full-out this time and Tarik was reminded of the grin on the king cobra right before it struck. "Do not concern yourself, my dear. It is nothing. My man will see you and the sheik to your room now. But please do join us for a late lunch at the pool."

Jass laughed and shrugged a shoulder. "I'll try. But I cannot guarantee an appearance from Sheik Zohdi. He is, what was it you said? No play but all work? That is why I am acting as his agent for the auction."

Eltsin gave an elegant wave of his hand. "The auction is two days away yet. In the meantime, I do hope to see you later. Until then?"

Jass nodded pleasantly and they took their leave, following the henchman up the staircase. Tarik could feel her trembling beside him, though her head was high and her chin strong. He wanted to wrap his arm around her shoulders to give her added strength. But he didn't want to call attention to her distress—or give her the idea he thought she was weak in any way.

No one on the outside would ever have guessed how difficult that scene must've been on Jass. He certainly hadn't noticed until now.

He hung back, leaned over and whispered in her ear. "Was the Ruger your only weapon?"

"Was the Walther yours?"

"Not a chance."

"Me neither." She'd made the reply in her own hushed tone as a twinkle appeared in her eyes. "What do you say we find someplace private and I'll show you mine if you show me yours?"

A chuckle escaped his lips. What better partner could he have than Jass? She, who joked in the face of danger.

Now all he had to do was keep her safe. From Eltsin. From the Taj. And most of all, from himself.

Chapter 10

"What if they've already been through our luggage?" Jass raised her voice to be heard from the closet while she removed the derringer from under her dress.

Tarik had finished checking their room for bugs and cameras and declared the place clean. Now he was rifling through her duffel and his briefcase in the bathroom.

"I'm sure they made a cursory inspection, but they didn't have the time to uncover what I hid.

It would take a better man than anyone Eltsin's got to find…"

As she ducked out of the closet, Tarik stepped out of the bathroom, assembling a revolver. "All the weapons we're carrying now are made of special plastic and won't show up on any metal screening. Don't be surprised to find ammo in with your underwear."

"You broke the weapons down into pieces?"

He grinned like a Cheshire cat with a bowl of milk. "Sure. A barrel in with the swimsuits. A grip in my briefcase with my laptop. A firing pin in with shaving cream."

Shrugging, he went on, "It's not hard to disguise and smuggle weapons if you know what you're doing and have the proper equipment."

"No wonder that duffel is so heavy. I've done the same kind of thing with the surveillance toys Ed supplied. I'm surprised the luggage doesn't clank when it's carried."

"Plastic, remember?" Tarik's face suddenly sobered. "Do you think your handler knows where we are? Could he have followed us?"

The smile spread across her face as she prepared to give up the secret she'd been carrying. "He knows. I'm tagged."

"What? They implanted a GPS on you? Where is it?"

"It's a chip no bigger than a grain of rice and it's right under the skin in a spot that's— Well, let's say you'd never notice the mark."

The thought of him touching her there, or maybe putting his lips to her skin over that spot, gave Jass an unwanted chill. But she swore not to let it lead to something more.

Yes, the man gave her serious chills—and then made her hot enough to sweat bullets. But he was only a partner on the job. A good partner, she was coming to believe. But not the kind of man she'd ever imagined falling in love with. He was a player—and a man who gave up on his sensitive job with the United States government in order to prove a theory she still wasn't completely convinced could be true.

Her father would never have done such a thing. He was her gold standard of behavior. No one else had ever measured up.

Besides, she wasn't looking for a relationship. Her career was far more important to her than throwing caution to the wind and having a good time in bed.

Oh, but she had a feeling Tarik could provide a woman with a real good time.

"Well, using your own words," he said with one of his whimsical smiles and raised eyebrows, "I'll show you mine if you show me yours."

"You're chipped, too? By whom?"

He lifted his arm and pointed to a spot under his armpit that was currently hidden by his shirt. "My brothers and I each carry a chip under the skin. Our operations people came up with the idea in order to keep track of where we were going. It's been a lifesaver on several occasions."

"So the Kadirs know where you are now?"

"I hope so. My brother Shakir should be in the area by now. I'm counting on him being close enough if we need his help."

That meant he could probably contact his people somehow.

Deciding not to ask him about communications yet, Jass posed another more pertinent question. "You didn't see any of the other guests when we were coming in, did you? I didn't. I wonder who the other bidders are and if they're here already, too."

"They're here. But no, I didn't see anyone on the way in either. Are you confident you know what's going to be up for auction?"

"It must be the fissionable material like on the file I found on the computer in Eltsin's office." After she'd posed the theory, the expression on Tarik's face led her to believe otherwise. "Why? What do you think?"

He tilted his head noncommittally. "The 'fissionable material' notation you saw was probably a red herring. And if you say anything about it, Eltsin will know it was us in his office."

She blew out a breath. "Good point. Do you have any suggestions for finding out what we're after?"

"I want to do a little snooping around. Maybe I can figure it out."

"And that's why you made such a point with Eltsin about your privacy and working from your room." What a terrific partner he made. The man could think on his feet far better than anyone she'd ever seen. "I take it you have a plan for scouting the area without being noticed?"

"Maybe. But I'm counting on you to keep Eltsin and the other guests occupied. Or at least be in a position to warn me if they're coming back to this wing of the house."

"I believe I have an idea for handling such a diversion." She could think on her feet fairly well, too. "But first I want to give you a quick lesson on the toys I brought along. Some of the surveillance equipment could prove useful for a snoop."

Tarik nodded and winked at her. "Okay, boss lady. I'm ready for instruction."

She sniffed at the term he'd used. Things had changed in her mind. They were partners. Neither of them was the boss of this operation.

But rather than raise a fuss, she retrieved her duffel and dragged it onto the desk. She turned back to him, ready with a dose of his own medicine.

For the first time in her entire life, she winked at a man. "Okay, class. Get ready to listen up."

Good God. Tarik felt his body go rock hard when Jass walked out of the closet a little while after their lesson dressed in the smallest damned thong bathing suit he had ever seen. And damned if it wasn't neon lime-green.

"What…" He choked on his own tongue. "Uh, what the devil do you think you're doing in that…that…thing?"

"*This* is a Brazilian-style bathing suit, not a thing. And it's part of my plan to keep the men busy while you scout around upstairs."

"Uh…" *Down boy.* "Yeah, I'd say your suit will capture everyone's attention all right. But where's your weapon hidden?"

"Not carrying one. But I'm not worried. I can take care of myself."

"Hope so," he grumbled under his breath.

"What?"

"I said I hope you can take care of yourself because you'll be fighting the men off like flies around a garbage dump."

Jass scowled. "Nice analogy, pal. How I dearly love being compared to a smelly landfill. That's a new one."

He wouldn't tell her what he truly thought about how she looked. She looked good enough to eat and he wasn't at all happy about terrorists, or any male, drooling over her nearly nude body.

He tried to remind himself she was only his partner, not a love interest like Celile was for Zohdi. And that this plan was part of her job, not a plan to make him jealous. Tarik fought to keep from demanding she cover up.

Instead, he said, "Do you think Sheik Zohdi would ever allow Celile out of his sight dressed in something like that?"

"No way." She rolled her eyes, turned and disappeared back into the closet.

A minute later she reappeared, shoving her arms through a wraparound dress. "I brought this beach cover-up along to make the sheik happy." She grinned at him.

The dress wasn't much better. Made out of some flimsy, see-through material with green and blue swirly patterns, nothing of importance was obvious underneath the so-called dress. But that only made it worse somehow. Male imaginations would run wild instead.

Tarik narrowed his eyes. "It's still…" At a loss for words, he waved a hand in the air.

"Isn't it just." Jass laughed and twirled around, letting him see her from all sides. "Still no place for a weapon. But this should do to keep Eltsin and his male guests' attention focused somewhere else besides on you. Don't you think?"

God help him, she was right. He didn't like it. Hated the idea, in fact. But it would probably work.

"When are you going to execute this plan of yours?" Tarik hoped her answer would be tomorrow or maybe the next day. *Never* would've been his first preference.

But she said what he'd feared. "In a moment, if you're ready to do your job."

The words didn't want to leave his mouth, but he pushed them out with a groan. "Ah…I'm ready. I guess."

Jass ducked back into the closet but almost instantly reappeared having added a pair of sexy, lime-green stiletto heels and a pair of sunglasses to the outfit. "Okay then. Me, too."

Tarik groaned again and swiped a hand across his suddenly dry mouth. Damn, she was hot.

This operation wasn't turning out the same way he'd had in mind. He'd pictured her in a black catsuit and him in his NVGs, riffling through computer files and listening in on conversations together.

Now the two of them would be going in alone. But, he knew part of his mind wouldn't be concentrating on the job. Not with the constant worry over how Jass was faring on her end.

Hell. He slammed one fist into the other and Jass raised her head in surprise.

"You okay?"

"Fine." If...he could manage to control his raging out-of-whack emotions and get back in the game. "I'll give you fifteen minutes to get down by the pool. If Eltsin isn't there yet or if anything else looks amiss to you, send a pool boy or valet up here with a drink for Zohdi. I'll abort."

"Right." Jass turned and headed out the door. "Be careful," she called as the door closed behind her.

Swamped with jealousy and tingling with desire, Tarik fought to maintain some semblance of control. His unsuitable responses to a female partner were simply becoming over-the-top and crazy as hell. He was acting more like a man in love than a man on a mission.

It wasn't as if he'd never worked with covert female operatives before. But somehow Jass was different than all the rest.

He thought again of her in that teeny, tiny

bikini and felt his pulse begin to race. Yeah. She was a lot different.

Damn it.

Jass lifted her chin and purposefully strode down the staircase one foot in front of the other, swinging her hips. Once on a long-ago sting, she'd portrayed a European swimsuit model, and she tried to put her mind back in that place and time.

But it was tough going when images of Tarik kept creeping into her consciousness and throwing her off-balance. The man was seriously hot. With her next step, she found her imagination transporting her back to last night when he'd been naked, wanting and hard as a rock.

Forced to put a hand on the banister now, she tried to steady herself as mental pictures of those broad, supple shoulders of his holding her down caused her to miss a step. His extraordinary chest had pinned her to the bed, while his lean hips and broad thighs had moved suggestively between her legs.

She'd felt his erection. Hot and pulsing. Exactly where she'd needed to feel it the most.

Stopping to take a breath, Jass ordered herself to quit daydreaming this instant and pull it together.

She had work to do. Important work that might mean life or death for Tarik.

Someplace along the line, the idea of putting her own career in high gear with this mission had begun to pale against the idea of helping Tarik prove his family's accusations. His mission had worldwide implications. Her career could hold for another day.

Yeah, he still irritated her to no end sometimes. The grin. The casual attitude masking a much deeper conviction. It all drove her nutty.

Worse, her own reactions to him on an intense, sexual level constantly made her angry with herself. Why now? Why suddenly find an unavailable and totally unsuitable man so attractive that she lost her mind whenever he was around? It didn't make sense.

"Ah, Ms. Kocak, is it?" A Middle Eastern–looking man hailed her as he came around the corner from the other wing of the house. "We've not had the pleasure of meeting. The name is Malik Kasim Taj Zabbar. I understand we are to be competitors at the auction."

Oh my god, this guy was one of the men at the table in Monte Carlo. Tarik and the Kadirs had been correct and the Taj Zabbar were seeking some kind of weapon of mass destruction. Of course, simply showing up for an auction was not conclusive proof to take to the international community. But it was good enough to make Jass a true believer.

Hoping to heaven her disguise would hold up under his scrutiny, she took the hand he held out. "The pleasure is all mine." Giving him a flirty gaze through her lashes, she squeezed his hand suggestively. "Are you representing yourself? Or an absentee buyer? I've found it pays to get to know your competition—very well."

He tilted his head as he studied her with a sober expression. "I am but a humble servant. And you, madam, are not the casual flirt that your expression and attire would suggest."

Oh, crap. "Me? But I am—"

"Please. Your title as the Messenger is well known and respected the world over. You are reputed to be a shark in the arms negotiations business." Malik tsked at her. "Do not try to fool me with your sweet smile and a stunning body. Let us begin on more equal footing—as true opponents."

Her whole body wanted to cave in with relief. He still believed she was Celile.

She pulled her hand free from his and set her jaw in true Celile style. "Agreed. I will be representing Sheik Abu Zohdi in this matter. Whom do you represent?"

He gave her a half smile. "Better. But I already knew your buyer. And I have to say Zohdi may not have the wherewithal to compete effectively. At least not with the resources of the new nation of Zabbarán behind my bids."

Man, she sure wished she had a digital recorder getting this conversation down. But there hadn't been any place to hide one. Tarik would have to find something else to incriminate these bastards.

And she needed to shift the current conversation out to the patio right this minute. Her job—and Tarik's life—might depend on her keeping an eye on all the others who should be out at the pool by now. Especially Eltsin.

She nodded her head and slipped her arm through the Taj Zabbar agent's arm, swinging him around and moving them both in the general direction of the patio. "We shall see, Malik.

Um, it is all right for me to call you Malik since we'll be such close competitors, isn't it?"

"Of course. If I might also call you Celile."

Oh, you bet yer boots, babes. "That will be fine. But please don't use my given name around Zohdi. Not if you care about living long enough to place your bid, that is."

After hiding their weapons and equipment around the room and waiting a full fifteen minutes, Tarik changed into a black T-shirt and jeans and began scouting the rest of the residential wing. It didn't take him five minutes to befriend one of the uniformed valets, who spoke Spanish instead of Portuguese and didn't seem to think asking detailed questions about the other guests was strange.

Sure enough, Tarik discovered several of the others were also Middle Eastern like he was. The valet even pointed out a couple of rooms belonging to men whose last names were both

Taj Zabbar, though he added the two weren't brothers.

After their conversation, Tarik followed the valet and uncovered a treasure trove. A large linen closet containing not only freshly washed and stacked towels and bed linens but also freshly washed valet uniforms. It didn't take him thirty seconds after the valet left to slip into a uniform and grab a handful of towels. He was headed back down the hall toward the first of the Taj's rooms before the valet was even out of sight.

Using a new high-tech master set of keys Jass's handler had provided, he got through the locked door a lot faster than if he'd had to rely on obsolete lock picks. The first thing he did was set the towels in the bath and then scour the bedroom for any hidden surveillance devices. He'd been ready to believe the Taj might even try to protect themselves by setting up some way of checking who entered their rooms.

But the place was clean. Not for long, though.

He put a listening device in both the bedroom and the closet, in case. While he was in the closet, he checked the safe but decided it would take too long to open it. The room itself held nothing of interest. No files, PDAs or laptops.

Were those things in the next room over? He grabbed up the old towels and replaced them with new ones as he prepared to leave. But when he opened the outer door, he heard voices coming from down the hall—and drawing closer.

Maybe he'd get lucky and it wouldn't be the Taj returning to their rooms. He stood at the threshold long enough to know it was not his lucky day. The male voices were speaking quietly in the Taj Zabbar language. He even recognized them as the same men from the club the other night.

Closing the door and locking it behind him, Tarik glanced around the room looking for someplace to hide. The drapes had been pulled, but hiding behind drapes was far too obvious.

He dashed back into the bathroom, wondering if he could pull off playacting as the real valet in front of the Taj Zabbar. Quickly deciding that would be pushing his nonexistent luck too far, his frantic glance landed on a tiny window in the shower enclosure and at the deep bathtub, half-hidden by frosted glass. He made a leap for the tub—at the exact moment someone entered the bedroom.

Chapter 11

Jass paced the floor of their room, fighting the urge to bite her nails—a habit she'd shed as a teen. Tarik had disappeared to heaven only knew where. A little while ago she'd noticed the two Taj Zabbar men leaving the patio for their rooms and had instantly sent the pool boy up with a drink for Zohdi. But the boy had come back within minutes claiming no one answered the door.

Where the hell was Tarik? Had the Taj caught him snooping in their rooms? Was he in danger somewhere and in need of her help?

Damn it, the two of them should have a better way of communicating if they were going to keep working separately.

Nearly frantic and too hyped up to think clearly, Jass began to wonder if she shouldn't go looking. She ripped the beach cover-up over her head and threw it toward the bed. Not sure what the proper attire would be for snooping around Eltsin's huge mansion, she untied the straps to her halter and slipped out of it. Catsuit or Celile disguise? Holding the scrap of material loosely in her hand, she headed toward the closet, still wondering what to put on.

At that moment she heard a sound. Muffled and indistinct, the noise sounded like someone scraping on a faraway door. But why could she hear it from here? She and Tarik had checked the acoustics of the rooms earlier and discovered you couldn't hear a thing from directly outside the door. The walls between rooms were also insulated far better than most five-star hotels.

Jass moved to the hall door and listened, in case someone was trying to break in. But the sound wasn't coming from that direction.

The scratching noise had to be coming from right outside the windows. But right outside the windows they were three stories off the ground. Was someone washing windows? Did this have anything to do with Tarik?

She went closer to the sliding glass door leading to their own tiny private balcony and peeked out past the heavy drapes that had been drawn to block the heat from the sun. The knock came again, and when she peered down the balcony, she saw Tarik, kneeling at the door and working at the lock with one of Ed's high-tech toys.

Oh my God. She grabbed the drapes and ripped them back.

"Get inside before someone spots you."

Hissing with fright and wanting to remain quiet, she unlocked the latch and slid open the glass door.

Tarik stepped inside looking disheveled and obviously out of breath. "Thanks. I wasn't having much luck with that lock." He reached up and wiped the perspiration from his forehead.

She stood shaking her head at him. "What on earth are you wearing?" He was dressed like one of the valets—only he looked much better.

With the button-down shirt open, his T-shirt clung to his taut muscles. She ached to touch him.

Tarik shook his head too but held his forefinger up to his mouth to indicate he wasn't going to answer.

Then he narrowed his focus on her as flames suddenly jumped into his eyes. "The question is, my dear Celile, what are you wearing?"

Jass froze, belatedly remembering she still

held the top to her bathing suit in her hand. A shiver of sexual heat raced from her fingertips to her breasts. She closed her eyes, hoping he would disappear, or that a hole would open up in the floor and swallow her whole.

No such luck. When she opened her eyes he was blatantly watching. A hungry stare. She became painfully aware of her nipples hardening. Taking a breath didn't help. As her chest swelled, the look in his eyes took on an intense quality—like the wolf gazing at Red Riding Hood.

Her nipples grew even harder. She was in deep trou-ble.

The memory of the kisses they'd shared came back to haunt her. She licked her lips once and Tarik moved closer, pulling her into his arms.

"Don't say anything until I check the room for bugs again," he whispered as he searched her eyes.

What was he looking for in her eyes? Fear? Rejection?

She wasn't feeling either one. Lifting her mouth to his, she told him what she wanted with her lips and tongue.

He tightened his hold on her, mashing her breasts against his chest as he participated in the kiss in every conceivable way. This wasn't an act. It was an astonishingly realistic move from a flesh-and-blood man who wanted *her*— not Celile.

Tarik no longer hid behind the mask of someone else. He was for real. The moment was for real. And she'd suddenly discovered some part of herself that had been hidden away wanting now to come out and play. Play only with Tarik.

Pressing on her bottom with his broad, hot hand, he jammed her tightly against his erection. Then he hummed, deep in his throat, as if this was the sweetest experience of his lifetime. To her ears, his murmur sounded of longing and pleasure, so closely matching what she was experiencing that it almost brought tears to her eyes.

She wanted to move even closer. Yet there wasn't so much as a breath of air between them. Throwing one leg up, she wound it around his hips and tried to climb right inside his body. She couldn't seem to get enough of his taste, and wished he had a lot fewer clothes on. She was dying to rub her tongue all over his skin.

He broke their kiss and lowered his head to her throat, moving his mouth in wide-open abandon toward the base of her neck and the pulse beating wildly there. She rocked against his hard erection, growing ever more desperate for a release of her tension.

His hand slid between them then and his palm cupped her with erotic warmth. She gasped, ready to explode.

Suddenly, he stopped. Froze. And swore quietly under his breath.

Her desire flamed, and then burned out in a rush of vulnerability, confusion and finally embarrassment. She stepped away and tried to cover herself with her hands.

"Go take a shower, Celile." Tarik looked embarrassed too as he nodded his head toward the bathroom. "We'll talk later."

The bugs. The mission. All of what had been lost in her lust-filled haze came back with the splash of a prickly air-conditioned chill.

She was such an idiot. Turning on her heels, she dashed out of the room to the relative safety of the bathroom and slammed the door.

Breathing deep and rushing to turn on the hot water in the shower, Jass swore at her own stupidity. Yet with each breath of air, she realized Tarik had become more than a partner and a friend. He'd become her everything, all within a few days. Furthermore, if he ever made a move in her direction again, she would fall into his arms without a moment's hesitation.

The woman she had always thought she'd been, the woman cautious with her emotions, was now gone for good.

Tarik stumbled around the room, ripping off the valet's coat and searching for the bug-detection device.

Holy hell. What had hit him?

As he found the detector and began running it along the four walls and checking the house phone, he thought back to a few moments ago when his hands were roaming over Jass. It had been pure heaven when his tongue slid into the warm, honeyed depths of her mouth. Exploring. Taking her with a savage kiss. Holding her tighter. Kissing her harder and harder while his heart went off like a time bomb in his chest.

She was so sweet. Her breasts so beautiful and her lips soft. Her tight, rounded ass felt solid as he filled his hands with her flesh. Her whole exquisite body was everything a man could ever want. Then, when she'd wrapped one of her slim, toned legs around his waist, he'd completely lost his mind.

It took her gasping out a breath as he'd touched her and found her wet, to make him remember they could be the starring attraction on some bad guy's headphones at that exact moment. It was possible the Taj or one of Eltsin's men had entered the room while they were gone and planted bugs. Earlier Tarik had set a thread over the door as a trap and to let him know if their privacy had been breached while they were out of the room. But Jass had entered through the door first and ruined his trap.

So, he'd forced himself to stop one of the most intense sexual experiences of his life.

Now he was checking for bugs. But still felt overheated and remained harder than he'd ever been.

He couldn't shake the image of Jass, nipples

peaked and looking up at him with a combination of desire and vulnerability in her eyes. A potent look, it had turned his knees to mush and his brain to ash. And nothing short of making love to her would help.

But that wasn't going to happen. Couldn't happen. *Shouldn't...*

After silently declaring the room to be clean, Tarik lifted his head and listened to the water as it continued running in the bathroom shower. He *should* clear the bathroom too—to be safe.

After shucking the rest of his clothes, he went to the door and hesitated, leaning his forehead against the air-cooled wood. If he opened this door, what would she do? What did he want her to do?

He knew what *he* wanted. He wanted to touch her again. And to run his mouth and tongue along every inch of that perfect body. She wanted that too, he was almost positive.

The indecision and options were killing him.

Making a deal with himself, a deal with the devil in his soul, he finally decided to try the door handle. If he found it unlocked, then that meant Jass had deliberately left it open as an invitation. If the door was locked, he would turn away, satisfied she had left him a message that she didn't want him.

Holding his breath, Tarik's hand closed around the handle. What would come next?

The door opened with a tiny squeak of hinges. He stepped into the room with his heart jackhammering in his chest. Shower steam clouded his vision, but it didn't keep him from seeing Jass looking out at him through the glass enclosure. Another moment of indecision had him blinking and swallowing hard. She had yet another shot at turning him down.

But as he closed the door and took a step toward her, she opened the shower door and held out her hand to him. She looked beautiful. Hot. He could weep with joy.

Physically, she was perfect. But it was the look in her eyes, saying she felt as hungry for him as he felt for her, that knocked him back a step. This exquisite and strong woman knew what she needed. And it threw him to find that what she needed was him.

More than anything, he needed to make love to her and watch her come apart in his arms. To pull down the moon and put that glow in her eyes whenever she looked at him.

The vulnerability he'd seen on her face earlier had disappeared. The heat and the need were back, lighting up the hazel-green eyes of Jasmine O'Reilly—not Celile Kocak's dark browns.

Tarik knew for sure what, and definitely who, he wanted in his arms.

Stepping into the shower, he took her hand. "We're in the clear. No bugs."

She smiled up at him but didn't make a move.

"Are you sure?" he asked, with his heart in his throat.

Instead of answering, Jass moved closer, went up on tiptoes and without touching anywhere else, pressed her wet lips to his.

"Why me?" he gasped.

"Because I need you." As simple and as complicated as that.

He could no more have found the will to turn her away after that than he could have sprouted angel wings and flown out the window. Dragging her hard against him, he buried his hands in the wild tangle of her short auburn hair and kissed her again. A kiss that spoke of desperation and a surprising kind of trust.

Without question, he trusted her not to disappear from his life the way other women he'd cared about had, the same way his mother had. He needed Jass to trust him as well. It was important, not only for their mission, but for her well-being. He wanted her to feel a real emotional connection to someone who had nothing whatever to gain by caring.

Standing flush against him and throwing her arms around his neck for balance, she kissed him back with equal desire. The water cascaded down on their heads. He pushed his thigh between her legs, backing her away from the direct spray and up against the tile wall. Because he couldn't stand being close and not touching. And because he was growing more insistent by the moment. Skimming his fingers along her ribs, he thrilled to the touch of her soft-as-a-cloud skin. He let his fingers roam lower, until his greedy hands palmed the sweetest bottom in existence.

Meanwhile he kissed her neck, gently nipping and then soothing with his tongue. Sliding his lips across her chin to capture her mouth, he kissed her deeply, angling his head to get a better taste.

Perfect curves. Slick bare skin. He broke the kiss and took a half step back to take her all in. She was a goddess.

He knelt to worship her body, wrapping his arms around her thighs and burying his face in her belly. The loveliness and the feminine scent of her went to his head, steaming his senses. Warning himself to take it slow, he eased open her legs and pressed his tongue to the hot, wet center of her desire. Teasing her. Licking her.

She moaned, softly grinding her hips to give him access to her velvet folds. Then she tunneled her hands through his hair to hold him in place.

Nothing short of death would've moved him away. Not yet. Not when this was what he'd wanted since the first moment he'd ever laid eyes on her.

"Tarik." The sound of his name on her lips whispered like a tangible force through his brain.

She spread her legs a little wider and he used the opportunity to slip his fingers up inside. Tight. Wet. What a gift she was, turning him harder than ever and electrifying his every cell. Plying her with his tongue and loving every taste, he reveled in the way she kept holding him tighter and snugger to her. He listened as the tiny little catches in her throat came closer together.

Come apart for me, love. He badly wanted to feel her flying. To give her a small part of the fantasy she was giving to him. He needed desperately to be the man who took her higher than she'd ever been.

Her guttural murmurs grew rougher as she forced his name from her lips over and over. He continued pleasuring her, on and on, endlessly sliding his fingers in and out and teasing her with the tip of his tongue.

He lost track of time until she tensed underneath his hands and her murmurs grew to soft cries. But as he felt the contractions of her release rippling through her body, she spat out a curse.

Yeah, sweetheart. The climax of a lifetime.

Her knees buckled and he rose to his feet to hold her upright in his arms. "Okay?"

She leaned in, put her mouth to his ear and groaned, "More."

Mindlessly, he covered her open and pliant mouth with his own and filled a hand with her breast. *More.* The word echoed through his mind as he tweaked one of her nipples.

Her moans grew more insistent. His mind twisted and bent in response. He pushed her back against the wall, his body taut and out of control.

Wrapping his free hand under her thigh, Tarik lifted her leg around his waist. With his tongue in her mouth and a hand still on her breast, he drove into her.

How easy it was to have found a reckless

pleasure deep and true enough that he never wanted it to end. Like this. With this woman. For the rest of a lifetime.

He thrust into her. Higher. Deeper. Again and again. Her body drew him all the way inside when she moved her hips in time with his. The heat and the rhythm urged him toward the ultimate edge.

Diving deep inside her one final time, he was grateful to feel her coming apart along with him while the extreme pleasure blasted at his body with a fiery heat. Her gasping breaths were hot against his mouth. Perfect.

Breathing in heavy pants, he remained inside her, listening to the sounds she made deep in her throat. He could do this all night. Stay right here with her in his arms.

Finally, she rocked against him. Only the slightest of movements, but it sent shock waves careening through his veins.

He tightened his arms around her and nuzzled

her neck, breathing in her scent and savoring the wondrous sensations of the soft and limp body wrapped around his. Did they have to move? Would either of them make it to the other room if they did?

"Oh, Tarik. That was so good." She ran her fingers through his hair and as she sucked on his earlobe.

She was the most responsive, giving woman he had ever encountered. No one else would ever come close to matching her in the future.

The ramifications of that thought had yet to sink in. They were only vague ideas, little ripples of unease in his subconscious mind. Later. He would give them further consideration later.

Slowly, and with more care than he thought he had in him, he pulled out of her. Lifting her in his arms, he reached around and flipped off the water. He stepped from the shower and, kissing her full on the mouth, carried her to bed.

Again, was all he could think. Under him. Surrounding him. Hovering over him while she rode him to bliss. Until they both went mad.

He wanted her again. And again.

Chapter 12

Jass sat upright against the headboard with the sheet pulled up under her armpits.

She glanced over at Tarik and found him asleep on his stomach, naked and stunningly male. And still looking good enough to make her head spin after two hours of lovemaking.

Golden skin and long black lashes gave his face an almost beautiful quality. The dark hair covering his chest ran down across tight abs and a flat stomach. Sleek and sinewy legs plus a good, strong butt drew her attention, holding her gaze immobile until she thought she might go cross-eyed. Raking her glance upward, she focused on his full head of tousled dark brown hair that had the sweetest way of curling along the edge of his neck. Her fondest wish was to never stop gazing at the man exactly like this.

But she could just imagine how *she* looked. No makeup. Sweat-dampened hair sticking up in spikes from Tarik running his fingers through it. Eyes probably a little bloodshot from her pulse rate soaring over the moon every time he made her come.

But Tarik hadn't seemed to mind how she looked. He'd held her and cared for her and gazed into her eyes with such hunger that he didn't even need to touch her in order to send her sailing.

And, dear God, she wanted him to do it over and over again.

One look at him brought on a rush of pure arousal. She dragged her eyes away and stared straight ahead. For now she needed to put her head back together and shape up. What had taken place between them had to be set right.

They were partners. Though how would they ever be able to work together again?

She couldn't look into his eyes now and pretend to see Sheik Abu Zohdi. Tarik would never touch her again without her seeing images of what they'd done; the way his clever fingers had touched her and his tongue had been compelling and erotic.

If she told Tarik nothing like that could ever happen between them again, would he pay attention? Maybe not. Would her own mind listen to reason? Probably not.

Desperate to find a solution to the dilemma she saw ahead of her, she tried a little rationalization. Asking herself if only one spectacular afternoon in bed could possibly make for a forever relationship, she determined that she wasn't a casual love 'em and leave 'em person.

Tarik seemed more the explode and burn type rather than the steady, ever-after hero of her dreams. He was all fireworks and flames—for a time. Judging by his staying power in bed… perhaps a long time. But he wasn't someone who could make her happy over an entire life-time. Was he?

He couldn't be her type. He was far too casual and easygoing. Almost too accommodating. Yes, it was nice having someone show such concern over her welfare. He'd been the most solicitous lover she'd ever had. Waiting until she was satisfied before—well, before satisfy-ing himself. But…how many others out there in the world also thought he cared only for them?

The idea that dozens of other women could be waiting for him to return was exactly the jerk on her chain she'd been needing to move her to action. Shoving the sheet back, she swung her feet over the side of the bed and stood.

As naked as the day she was born, she felt

someone watching her and turned around to find Tarik's eyes open and a huge grin creasing his face. "You okay, love?"

"Stop that." She turned her back on him and found her robe. But she could still see him in the mirror.

"Stop what?" He sat up and leaned on his elbow, watching her shrug into the sleeves.

"Number one: Stop calling me *love* in private. You don't know me well enough for gooey stuff like that. We're partners on a mission. Period."

The silly grin never faltered.

"And number two: Stop asking me if I'm okay. I'm a big girl. If I wasn't okay, I would speak up and tell you so."

"Sorry. But you can't put the genie back in the bottle, *partner.*" Tarik tilted his head as his eyes softened. "Why don't we discuss this later? Right now, come back to bed."

The gorgeous bastard actually had the nerve

to hold out his hand as though he expected her to obey and blindly fall all over him.

"We're partners," she insisted. "What happened can't happen again. This is a mission, not playtime."

That broke the grin and brought him up out of the bed in one fluid motion. "Number one," he ground out as he headed around the bed in her direction. "We're undercover as lovers on this mission. Zohdi and Celile will be kissing, touching and in bed together again before we're finished with the job."

He reached for her and pulled her into his arms as she tried to step back. "And number two—" His dark gaze pinned her with steely intent. "You think we can ignore the raging passion between us for the rest of this mission? I believe you're wrong, but let's say you're right. I promise you that *after* the mission, we will be revisiting not only what happened between us, but also this whole conversation. Take those words to the bank."

She opened her mouth to disagree, but he leaned in and hungrily glued his mouth to hers. As they tangled their tongues together, he clutched her hips and dragged her close. She'd already noticed how hard he was again, how much he wanted her. Now she felt the truth. It was impossible to miss. Her body yearned to take him in, to welcome him right back inside where she wanted him to stay.

Taking a breath, she murmured against his lips, "Why me? Why now?"

He pushed her away and ran a hand through his hair. "I don't know why this had to happen now. But I do know *why you*. Because you're important. Because...we fit."

She was speechless as her eyes filled with tears. They did *fit*, but what the hell was she supposed to do about that?

As he reached for her again, the room phone

rang. Both of them jerked around to stare at the offending object as if it were a king cobra.

Tarik snagged the receiver and murmured something she couldn't make out. He spoke a few more soft words in the broken English of Sheik Zohdi while she tightened the robe around her waist.

After he hung up, he ignored her and went to the closet. "We're expected downstairs for dinner in an hour."

The mission. Her head went back into the game in a flash. "I had supposed they would skip dinner altogether tonight. It's late."

"It's only ten." When Tarik reappeared he was wearing his robe and had a tiny laptop in his hand. "We're in South America, remember."

Yeah, she was having a hard time remembering anything since he'd kissed her to the point of delirium and told her she was important.

Tarik set the laptop up on the desk and hit a few keys. All of a sudden a vaguely familiar voice came through the speaker. It was the Taj Zabbar agent who'd stopped her on the stairs. She would never forget that gravelly voice. What was he saying?

After about a half an hour of listening to drivel while the two Taj Zabbar agents argued in their own language, Tarik finally heard something worthwhile.

"I told you before not to concern yourself with the other bidders." Malik Kasim, head of Taj secret police, was not happy with his underling.

Tarik had no trouble translating the words he was receiving from the device he'd planted in the agent's room. What he was having trouble with was getting his mind and body back under control. Still hungry for Jass and becoming more frustrated by the second, he clamped down on his teeth and forced the delectable image of her in the shower out of his head.

Malik continued haranguing his counterpart. "All of this…the dinner, the supposed auction on Tuesday. All of it is for show." He drew a breath and clicked his lips. "Finish packing our bags. We leave here before morning."

"But, Excellency, Eltsin told the woman she had as good a chance as any of making the winning bid. I heard him."

"Stop being such a fool. Once more, there will be no bids. Eltsin has already sold me a piece of what we came here seeking. As soon as he verifies our cash has been deposited to his bank later tonight, we will have everything we need."

"But the others…?"

"While we disappear with our prize, the other supposed bidders will be eliminated. It is part of our deal with Eltsin."

Dead air came through the listening device as the other man apparently questioned his boss without words.

"Our deal with Eltsin," Malik repeated with force. "No one leaves here who can identify us or make any connection to the Taj Zabbar."

Tarik listened another minute or two, but all he heard was Malik leave the other man with instructions on what to wear and when to appear downstairs. Shutting down the receiving device, Tarik stashed it away. He needed to talk to his brothers. Was Shakir nearby?

"What were they saying?"

He gazed up at Jass and his chest burned with the pain of how beautiful she looked. "Get dressed. And pack whatever you think you'll need for a quick departure."

She came closer. "Talk to me. Tell me what's going on."

How could he tell her she was already marked for death because of the parts they were playing? It wouldn't happen of course. He wouldn't let it. But he was having trouble forming the words.

"You just told me I was important. If that's true, if you think of me as more than a partner, then tell me what you overheard. Was it about whatever is supposed to be auctioned off?"

Shaking his head, he swallowed the unwarranted fear gripping his gut and thought only about Jass being a professional covert agent. "The Taj Zabbar are preparing to leave later tonight. They were talking about Eltsin killing off the rest of the bidders after they go."

Instead of fear or even apprehension in Jass's eyes, he saw understanding and determination. Inexplicably his chest swelled with pride. *There you go, my covert love.*

"The auction is a ruse, then," she said almost to herself while she shook her head thoughtfully. "Of course it would be. But Eltsin has a lot of nerve to off Celile and Zohdi. It'll ruin his reputation for any arms business he might want to do in the future."

"I suspect he'll be getting paid enough from the Taj that he won't mind."

"Must be liberating to control that much money." Jass shrugged a shoulder. "Or very seductive. Money can be the ruination of otherwise decent people."

He nodded.

"Sad but true."

"So what's your plan?" she asked.

"One of my brothers and a few men are supposed to be standing by. Probably in the forest within sight of Eltsin's mansion right now. We need a way out of here and a way to follow the Taj." He breathed deeply. "Plainly, we need help, and I don't think we can wait until the local CIA troops make it up here."

"Agreed. But how do you intend to reach your brother? Part of our instructions were not to use the internet or wireless communications while inside Eltsin's compound. He could easily intercept any of those kinds of signals and kill us without a second thought."

"True." He went into the closet to check the weapons and his Zohdi suit, still capable of talking to Jass without seeing her. "I have to find a way to step outside the mansion walls alone. Maybe into the patio and pool area while everyone else is in the dining room?"

"Hmm."

Okay, he needed to see her face. That didn't sound good.

Sticking his head out the closet door, he watched as she put a thoughtful finger to her chin and tapped a foot on the carpet. "What's going on in that tricky little mind of yours?"

"Little mind?" She gave him a joking smile but raised her eyebrows as if she were truly questioning his words.

"Come on, give. You know what I meant."

"Yeah, I know. And I think I have a plan."

She started toward him. "But there's one major problem to work out first."

He leaned back as she brushed past him into the closet. "What's that? Maybe I can help."

She started digging through Celile's clothes. "I'll tell you all about it in a minute. Right now you would only slow me down. I have to decide on the right thing for Celile to wear. That's going to be the key."

With her head held high, Jass strode into Eltsin's huge, gilt-edged dining room on Tarik's arm. She knew her partner still wasn't crazy about her plan. But it *would* work, and he had finally agreed that it was all they had.

On their way across the foyer, she'd stashed a collapsible backpack with their weapons and a change of clothes behind a mahogany grand-father clock decorated with gold leaf details and hand-tooled scrolls. The clock was one big, ugly son of a gun, but it would be stable when she was in a hurry. And it stood close to the front doors, where she could grab the pack on the fly.

Tarik, in his Zohdi suit and thick head scarf, had armed himself to the teeth with concealed weapons. But his most important accessories were the communications devices he'd planted in both his ears and then covered with the white cloth.

She knew he'd been concerned about the Taj showing up for dinner and getting a good look at his face. It was a chance they had to take. If her plan worked the way she hoped, no one was going to be paying much attention to Zohdi before he left the house anyway.

As they walked into the dining room, fashionably late, Eltsin was standing near the door, speaking quietly to the Taj Zabbar agents. All three men had drinks in their hands. She couldn't make out their words, but everyone stopped speaking and turned to stare at her and Tarik as they came closer.

The expressions on the men's faces were plain enough. The Russian and the two Taj agents silently gazed at them as though they were looking at two dead men walking. Or one dead man and one dead woman, as the case may be.

Shivering through the thin linen jacket she'd worn, Jass resisted the temptation to run. She would've preferred to wear a nice pair of jeans and running shoes for a quick getaway later. But that would not have worked well with her plan. Instead, she stabilized on her four-inch spike heels.

"Good evening," Eltsin mumbled at last. "We've been waiting for you to arrive. Would you care for a drink before we sit down to table?"

Tarik kept his mouth shut. He was still worrying about the Taj recognizing him under his disguise. But that was okay, because his supposed angry silence would match her plan quite well.

She dropped Tarik's arm and moved closer to their host. "I'm so sorry we're late, Mr. Eltsin. Forgive us. We…uh…the Sheik and I were having a slight disagreement upstairs."

"We're serving *caipirinhas* this evening," Eltsin said formally. "They're delightful. Can I interest you in joining us?"

"Why yes, drinks sound lovely."

The Taj agents remained silent in the corner as Eltsin turned to a servant and took a couple of drinks off a silver tray. He handed one to Tarik and then turned to hand one to her. When he did, the deadly look that had occupied Eltsin's eyes before suddenly became a creepy leer.

"You look magnificent tonight, Celile. In the past I have heard much about your reputation in business. But I never heard anything about how beautiful you were. Welcome." He lifted his glass in toast to her.

She lifted her glass too and gave him the most come-hither look she could manage. Toughest part of her job.

"Why, thank you." She even forced herself to bat her eyelashes at the bastard.

Tarik stepped closer to both of them, turning his back on the Taj Zabbar. He cleared his throat to notify Eltsin of his presence.

Jass pretended to take a sip, ignoring Tarik. She even inched slightly to one side, lifting her shoulder to close Tarik out of the circle of the conversation.

"This is delicious." She laid a hand on Eltsin's chest. "But doesn't it seem too warm in here? Would you mind holding the drink for me while I remove my jacket?"

Eltsin's leer became more pronounced. "Of course, my dear. Would you like to have the fans turned on? We don't want you to be uncomfortable."

"Don't trouble yourself." She pulled off the jacket, revealing the silky halter top and matching tight skirt she'd worn.

Tarik hissed out a breath and reached for her arm. "Dress yourself, Celile."

She reared her arm back and gave him a small shove with the other. "Don't tell me what to do, Zohdi."

Tarik spat out a curse in Arabic, something about her burning in a thousand hells, and threw the liquid in his glass at her chest. "Cover up!"

"Ahhh. Damn." Jass's specifically chosen top immediately became see-through. Instead of covering up, she narrowed her eyes at Tarik and threw back her shoulders. "How dare you? Get out of my sight, Zohdi. Now. Before it's all over between us."

"Gladly," Tarik said in Russian. Then he

pitched his empty glass against a wall and stormed from the room, being sure to keep his head down and allowing his face to remain concealed by the head scarf.

Jass made no attempt to cover up; instead she turned to Eltsin with a sheepish grin and her breasts clearly outlined beneath the sheer material. "I must apologize for the Sheik, Mr. Eltsin. He…he…" She sniffed and stepped in closer to Eltsin as though she would like to lean against his shoulder for support.

Both the Taj Zabbar agents walked closer to where she and Eltsin stood, shaking their heads solicitously.

"Would you like someone to walk you back to your room to change?" the Taj agent she'd met before asked.

Jass blinked and shook her head. "Thank you, but it's nothing. I'm fine this way." She threw her chest out and stood tall. "The material will dry soon enough. I wouldn't want to ruin your dinner."

The dinner you expect to be my last, you bastards.

Turning back to Eltsin, she glanced up at him with a shy smile. "You don't mind if I come to the table slightly damp, do you, Mr. Eltsin?"

The Russian dragged in a gulp of air and reached for her hand. "Not at all." Riveting his gaze on her chest, he gave her fingers a squeeze and then folded her whole hand between both of his in a too-familiar embrace. "Would you like me to send someone to bring back the Sheik?"

"Thank you, but no. He'll probably sulk outside in the fresh air for a bit, smoking one of his smelly cigars. No doubt he'll show up at the table in time for the dessert course. Do you mind entertaining me alone until then?"

Eltsin threw a quick glance at the Taj, then put his free hand around her shoulders. "Not at all. You are much prettier to look at than he is.

Let us see if we can't distract you over a meal until the Sheik returns."

Yeah? And exactly who is distracting whom here? she wondered with an imaginary roll of the eyes.

Go bring the cavalry to the rescue, Tarik.

Chapter 13

Tarik turned his back to the wind and lit one of the Padrón panatelas he carried as part of the Zohdi disguise. Smooth and complex, the limited-version cigar was a true cigar lover's brand. Not to his taste, but it would give him a good excuse for going off by himself and moving closer to the cover of the rainforest surrounding Eltsin's mansion.

Once he felt comfortably alone, Tarik noiselessly clicked open the comm to Shakir and whispered, "You nearby, bro?"

Shakir's deep voice flowed through the comm like a fine wine. "NVGs trained on your position. Location two hundred feet northwest in the tree tops. What's up?"

"All hell is about to break loose. Taj have secretly procured whatever they came to buy and are taking off later tonight for parts unknown. We need reinforcements."

"Got your back. Tell me what you need. We've been negotiating with one of Eltsin's henchmen for info on the Taj deal. Should have him opening up within the hour. And there's a scientist training his MASINT machines at Eltsin's place as we speak."

"A device for Measurement and Signature Intel on nuclear radiation? What's your geek gotten so far?"

"Nothing." Shakir made frustrated noises over the comm.

"Not surprised. I'm beginning to think that whatever is being traded here tonight, it's not another nuclear weapon. I haven't seen anyone who looked the least bit nervous or ill at ease as if they knew something radioactive was on the premises."

"Bloody hell." Shakir drew in a breath. "You have any other ideas about what's going down then?"

"No, but I do know it's something big. Eltsin gave the Taj agents his word he would eliminate all the other bidders once they were on their way out of the house."

"All the other bidders? As in Celile and Zohdi, too?"

"That's right," Tarik confirmed.

"Must be costing the Taj a pretty penny for that kind of promise. How much time have we got?"

"Not long. What I need from your team are eyes and ears trained on the Taj agents. I'll deal with Eltsin, but I don't want to alert the Taj to what we're doing. Someone needs to follow them. Preferably you." He sighed deeply. "See where they're headed. We can't lose contact with them. We have to find out what the Taj are planning before it's too late to stop. It's something huge. I can feel it in my gut."

"Right. I'll go down now to…uh…convince Eltsin's chauffeurs and any outside bodyguards that our men should be the drivers for the Taj when they leave. You want anything else?"

"A car gassed and ready to travel in a hurry might be nice."

"Your wish is my command. You…" Shakir seemed to hesitate about something, which was quite unlike his big brother. "You having any trouble with your partner?"

Tarik bristled but bit his tongue. "None. Why?"

"Someone overheard one of Eltsin's men talking about the sexy female. About how he'd been told not to touch, that she was special. Eltsin's private stock. You sure she's a hundred percent, bro?"

"Let me worry about Jass. You do your part and don't let the Taj out of your sight."

Shakir grunted a response. "Whatever you say. But watch out for yourself, brother. Things could go sour in an instant."

Tarik clicked off and ground his panatela into the wet earth, thinking about Jass. Eltsin's men were right about not messing with her. She'd as soon shoot their balls off as she would smile at them. But they didn't know that.

Why would Eltsin warn them off? It was possible he wanted her for himself. Or, perhaps Eltsin could have another agenda.

Was something else happening behind the scenes that Tarik didn't understand? Bouncing on the balls of his feet, he turned back to the main house, ready for anything.

He didn't see his attackers until they were already on top of his position.

"Come on, you assholes," he growled as he flipped the first man on his back and reached for his weapon. "Show me what you've got."

"Would you like an after-dinner drink with your dessert, my dear Celile?" Eltsin hadn't stopped leering at Jass since Tarik had left the table nearly an hour ago.

She was starting to itch. Most of the other guests had already retired. And the two Taj agents sitting beside her at the table also seemed ready to be on their way. They were about as fidgety as she was. Where was Tarik?

"Why yes, Mr. Eltsin, I would like another drink. Thank you." It was all she could do to sit still and smile.

Eltsin patted her hand and told the waiter to bring her whatever she required. "Please call me Andrei, Celile. It's a shame Sheik Zohdi has not returned to the table. But these gentlemen—" he gestured to the Taj agents "—and I have a little business we must attend to. It will only take a short while, but I dislike leaving you alone."

"Don't worry about me." She waved her hand as though she was already tipsy and not quite in control of her senses. "You gentlemen go right ahead."

She rose from her seat and all the men immediately stood, too. "If you don't mind, I may step out on the patio for a moment and see if I can find Zohdi while you're gone."

Eltsin's eyes took on a wary and dark expression. "All right, but don't go too far. Your lover doesn't deserve your concern. He doesn't seem to show you the same respect."

Jass nodded and deliberately stumbled.

"And stay on the patio." Eltsin made the demand in a harsh tone, but then seemed to think better of it. "I wouldn't want anything to happen to you. The jungle can be quite dangerous at night."

So can your mansion, my dear creep.

She put a hand to her breast and wobbled on her heels as though the idea was a bit daunting for a woman who'd had too much to drink. The elder of the two Taj agents came to her rescue and put his arm around her shoulders.

"Aren't you feeling well, Ms. Kocak?"

It was the perfect opportunity. The one she'd been waiting for. She slipped the microscopic GPS chip off her underarm and put her hand against the elder Taj's, pretending to steady herself. From that position, it was a snap to secretly paste the extra chip to the elder's wrist without him being any the wiser.

"I'll be fine," she told him with the imitation of a shy smile. "Do not worry over me. I simply need a little air. But I'll stay where I can see back inside this room. I'll know when you return to the table from your business."

She turned to Eltsin with wide eyes. "Surely

you will have another moment for me then, won't you, Andrei?"

"Count on it, Celile." Eltsin picked up her hand and kissed the fingertips. "Until then."

Ewww.

Eltsin and the Taj agents left the room. She watched them go. Then she weaved her way to the French doors leading to the pool area, still acting tipsy for any watchful eyes. She had a bad feeling about this. What if Eltsin had already ordered Tarik's execution? Her partner had been gone too long for comfort.

Jass hesitated at the patio door, while various scenarios raced through her mind. And then she turned to the nearest waiter.

Speaking to him in broken English, she said, "I'd like the use of a powder room before Mr. Eltsin returns. Is there one I can use that's closer than our room in the other wing?"

The waiter directed her toward the foyer, exactly where she'd hoped to go. Once she was near the grandfather clock, Jass checked over her shoulder. When convinced no one was watching, she dug into her backpack. Again thoroughly checking her surroundings inside the grand, shadowy foyer, she pulled out the phony cell phone that secretly doubled as a communications unit direct to her handler. If anyone spotted her, she would say she was trying to reach Zohdi on his cell.

This call was against orders, but she was sure the sting would soon be collapsing anyway. With the cell in her hand, she ducked into the powder room underneath the stairs and touched the button to raise Ed.

In less than two seconds, he answered. "Where are you?"

"Eltsin's mansion. But the sting's going south." She hated saying this to Ed; hated hearing the disappointment she knew would fill his voice. "Kadir is missing, and we're supposedly on Eltsin's hit list for later tonight. Something's bad with the whole deal. I need more men or we'll lose our chance at the Taj Zabbar."

"It'll take too long to put a force together." Ed's tone did not sound disappointed, nor even surprised. Yet her old friend sounded less than pleased. "Scrap the mission. Find a way out of the house and put miles between you and Eltsin as fast as you can."

"What about Kadir? I can't..."

"Leave him and get out. He's probably long gone by now."

"He might be in trouble," she said.

"Look, Jass, I told you the man has his own agenda. He wouldn't give you a second thought if your positions were reversed. Leave now."

Knowing her time was short, she didn't argue. She ended the conversation and cut the comm line to Ed without asking all the questions rolling in her mind. Standing still for one more second to think, she tried to focus on what to do next. She didn't believe for one moment that

Tarik would leave her to save himself. More than that, something in Ed's tone sounded way off.

Suddenly all the things that had been bothering her rushed to mind. But she was sure Tarik wasn't keeping anything from her. She'd come to know him, almost too well, over the last few days. And he'd been open and honest with her. Jass assured herself she couldn't care for him if he was anything but a good man. Her gut instincts on such matters had kept her alive many times in the past.

Yet, she was equally as sure that someone in this operation was betraying them. Someone she'd missed. First, the betrayal of the other night at Eltsin's office. And now she was having a bad feeling that Eltsin already knew she and Tarik were covert agents. The Russian was playing a much bigger and more deadly game with them than he let on. The tentacles of his operation must be far reaching. Maybe even into the local CIA?

She needed to find Tarik. Despite what she'd said to Ed, she had no doubt her partner was alive and in control of his situation. Maybe he'd managed to reach his brother and they were working out a plan.

Jass peered past the powder-room door and glanced into the adjoining room. She found the foyer and grand hall as quiet as when she'd come in. Eltsin should still be in his meeting with the Taj.

Now if she could make it through the front door without arousing any suspicions, she'd be free to scout around outside and locate Tarik. Together they would have no trouble overpowering Eltsin's guards and could come up with a way of stopping the Taj Zabbar. The most important part of the whole mission was not letting the Taj agents get away with their prize.

She tiptoed across the shadow-filled room,

snagged her backpack and opened the front door. But the telltale click of a silent security alarm alerted her to the glaring mistake she'd made before she could even set one foot outside.

Damn. The front door was armed. But there hadn't been any alarms on that door earlier. Eltsin must have been expecting some kind of move from them. Things were turning from bad to worse by the minute.

Feeling it was too late to turn back, and hearing the running footsteps closing in from behind her, she scurried outside into the sultry night. She couldn't outrun a turtle in these heels. Her best move had to be hiding.

Dashing to the left, Jass tried to stay within the shadows of the mansion while she headed for the forests. But almost instantly, glaring bright security lights lit up the entire night sky. *Rats.*

She wouldn't get another twenty feet before

Eltsin's men caught up. Her breathing labored and heavy from the tension, she squeezed into a blind alcove and leaned against a half-hidden stucco wall. Reaching into her backpack to pull out one of Tarik's specially made revolvers, she hefted it in her palm, getting the feel of a weapon that resembled her favorite Ruger .357 Magnum. Then she made sure the gun was loaded.

Now, which way would be her best bet?

Suddenly the sound of cars starting up caught her attention. The engine noises came from the garage area. Someone, probably the Taj Zabbar, was preparing to leave the mansion. She should stop them.

But her lone weapon was not going to get her far. And she was beginning to worry about Tarik—though she still felt certain he was holding his own.

Her best move for locating him would lie with finding the Taj. She imagined Tarik hiding somewhere near the garage side of the house. Maybe he was even waiting there for her help.

Determined to make the right move and not let herself get caught first, she stashed her backpack again and eased out of the alcove with weapon in hand. But she had hardly taken two steps when someone grabbed her by the shoulder and turned her around.

"Tarik!" She rounded on him and hissed, "You scared the life out of me. Was it you following me out of the house?" Lowering the gun, she took a deep breath and tried to calm her pounding heart.

"It was me. I've been looking for you." He had his hands on both her shoulders and was gazing at her with question in his eyes. "When I made it back to the dining room and found you gone…I…I…"

He'd been worried about her? Her first reaction was indignation. She was a pro, damn it. But the sudden flash of hurt to her pride only lasted a second or two before being replaced with a gooey, warm feeling that had nothing whatever to do with the mission or their jobs. And everything to do with the besotted look in his eyes as he stared deep into hers.

"I'm okay." She slipped out of his hold so as not to be distracted by either his warmth or those sexy, bedroom eyes. "But the Taj. I think they're getting away. Let's find a way of following them."

Tarik shook his head. "Shakir's handling the Taj. I want Eltsin. That Russian knows more than simply what was supposed to be sold here tonight. He knows a name. And he's going to give us that name."

Name? Tarik had been thinking the same thing that she had? "Yeah. I'd like the identity of the traitor, too. Let's go."

"Find a place to hide your weapon first." Tarik raked her up and down with an exasperated look before holding out his palms with a questioning expression in his eyes. "Well, do *something* with it. And fast. Surprise works a hell of a lot better than a full-frontal attack."

The game was over. But Tarik didn't want to think too long about who might be the traitor. It had to be someone connected to the Task Force, and the idea that someone he knew—someone he'd trusted—was in league with the Taj seemed so outrageous he refused to consider the possibilities.

He would wait and hear the name from Eltsin's own lips.

Meanwhile, Tarik fought his conflicting emotions over Jass. She was the smartest, most capable agent he'd ever encountered. But he wished he could shake the images of her naked—in the shower…in the bed…and in his dreams.

Earlier, even when they'd both been sated and exhausted, he'd laid across the bed trying to find enough reserve energy to do it again. He refused to close his eyes; he'd rather think about her and the way they'd fit together. Instead of gazing at her amazing body while she slept, he'd stared at the ceiling and listened to her breathe.

After most of a lifetime spent playacting as the chameleon, wanting people to love him for who they thought he was, he'd finally found someone who knew the real person underneath. And she actually cared for him anyway.

It felt as though he'd taken an emotional exhale.

She was...like coming home. There wasn't any other word but home that matched the feeling.

But Jass was not convinced. He'd seen it in her eyes. Deep down she felt scared. Afraid to take a chance with her emotions. She'd held herself apart from any real human contact for so long that she didn't know how to stop protecting herself from the possibility of being hurt.

That was no way for such a loving person to exist. He hurt for her. Hurt for the relationship she would eventually throw away. Yeah, he knew she wouldn't stick around forever. At least not physically. She was like a frightened rabbit who would run for the cover of her work at the first scary emotional moment.

But it would be harder for her to shake the memories of the two of them and the very real sense of belonging that they'd built over the past few days. They did belong together, damn it.

She couldn't forget that.

Nothing would happen to her while they finished the mission. He wouldn't let it. As tough as she was, the professional covert agent still needed him beside her to keep her safe. They were partners. And she wouldn't forget that either.

At the building's edge, Tarik halted with Jass right behind him and peered toward the garage area. The Taj were long gone. But the car Shakir had promised to leave sat in the open driveway, hopefully with the keys in the ignition.

Tarik had changed his mind since he'd last talked to his brother. After being attacked out beside the pool by a couple of Eltsin's incapable henchmen, he'd learned they already knew they were dealing with covert agents. But he hadn't learned how they knew. He'd made up his mind that when he and Jass left Eltsin's mansion in a few minutes to catch up with the Taj, Eltsin would be coming along.

And the Russian would sing his guts out, telling them all about how he'd known who they were.

Tarik gave a quick thought to the weapon he'd stuck in his waistband. It had originally belonged to one of Eltsin's men. Now it would be the tool he used to bring down Eltsin himself.

"We're going in through the kitchen area," he told Jass. "We can raise enough of a ruckus there that the kitchen help will call on Eltsin to come remove the guests. We'll ambush him as he enters the room. That's the only way to take him alive."

"I'm not sure about this plan," Jass whispered. "Where are all his gunmen? It seems too quiet out here. They should be looking for us by now."

"I'm sure we've already neutralized most of Eltsin's men. I took out a couple by the pool and Shakir probably took out the ones who were stationed outside near the garage area. Besides, this is the best plan we've got." He added one more thought for good measure. *"Trust me."*

Jass rolled her eyes, but nodded her head in agreement. "Okay. Let's go see if we can surprise the man who thinks he has all the answers."

Tarik had previously scoped out the kitchen entrance and knew most of the layout. Keeping to the wall, he took Jass by the hand and opened the servant's door to the pantry.

"Why isn't this door on the alarm system?" Jass wanted to know.

"Shush. The servants use this entrance and they probably keep the alarm turned off to make it easier for them to go in and out."

But by the time he and Jass entered the kitchen proper, Tarik's gut instincts were screaming in protest. Too quiet. The lights were dimmed and not one soul was still at work. The place was empty.

"Where is everybody?" Jass echoed his sentiments. "How are we going to make that *ruckus* of yours now?"

She was right. As Tarik reached for his

weapon, he nodded for her to turn back. They needed to get the hell out of here.

"There you two are." Eltsin's voice came from right behind them. "Drop the weapon, Sheik Zohdi, or whatever your name is. I've been expecting you."

Tarik swore under his breath. Bad move. But thank heaven he was already standing between Eltsin and Jass. She would have a better chance of staying alive if she hid behind him. Tarik bent and gently set the gun down on the tile floor.

"Good. Now slowly turn around to face me and then kick the gun in the other direction."

As Tarik raised his head and prepared to turn, he whispered to Jass, "Stay behind me."

"Right," she whispered in return. "When I say drop, you drop."

What? No. That wasn't what he'd meant at all. But it was too late for further debate.

"Come on," Eltsin demanded. "Stop the

whispering and do what I say. It would be a shame to have to shoot you in the back, but I will."

Grinding his teeth and drilling a look at her that clearly shouted "no way," Tarik forced himself to turn and kick the weapon out of range.

Jass stepped up so close behind him that he could feel her breath on the back of his neck.

"Trust me," she murmured.

Chapter 14

Trust. For days he'd been wanting her to trust him. Now he was faced with the reverse situation. But could he give her that much in return—without reservations?

"No. No." Eltsin waved his gun. "That's not the way I want you. Move out from behind him, Celile. You begin walking toward the dining room alone while I finish with Zohdi in here."

Ah. The Russian idiot actually thought he might kill off one covert agent and still have a chance at sex with the other? Tarik would've laughed in his face had the barrel of Eltsin's weapon not been pointed at the middle of his forehead.

"She's not going anywhere, Eltsin. You want her, you have to go through me."

"I will if I must. But I thought you might like a little information first. To satisfy your curiosity?"

Tarik could feel Jass rustling behind him, but she stood her ground and didn't move out in the open. *Good girl.*

"You don't have anything I want." Tarik folded his arms over his chest.

"Oh? Don't pretend you know what was being exchanged here tonight. Nuclear detonators? Child's play. You haven't the first idea of how our revolutionary new technology for nuclear delivery will change the world."

Nuclear delivery systems? Tarik unfolded his arms. Now he knew he needed to find a way of capturing this ass alive. For information.

"Ah. I see that has sparked your interest. Are you willing to do as I say? You've got less than a minute to decide."

"I'll do what you want, Eltsin." Jass called out in a clear voice, but she didn't move a muscle. "Just don't shoot him. Or you get nothing from me."

Eltsin's eyebrows shot up. "What's happened to your heavy accent, Celile?" Then the Russian smiled as he narrowed his eyes with a look that Tarik never wanted to see again.

This wasn't good. "I have another question, Eltsin." Anything to capture the man's attention. "Don't you…"

"Sorry, time's up." Eltsin raised his gun hand. *"Drop!"*

Tarik ducked and all hell exploded at once. Weapons fired. The smell of gunpowder assaulted his nose, and the too-close discharge of a weapon rang loudly in his eardrums, deafening him. He felt the sting in his upper arm and knew he'd been hit.

Cradling his painful right arm, Tarik fought to see through the clearing smoke. He couldn't hear anything. Couldn't see anything.

What the hell happened to Jass?

Cursing under her breath, Jass pulled her fingers away from the silent pulse point on Eltsin's neck. Dead cold. Damn bastard wouldn't take no for an answer. She'd known how much Tarik wanted to take him alive. But she couldn't let the Russian kill her partner simply to get at the truth, could she?

"Jass!" Tarik's panicky voice reached out and tugged at her heart.

She stuffed her weapon inside the waistband of her skirt and sought him out through the lingering gun smoke. In two steps she was kneeling beside him and searching for signs of where he'd been hit.

There was some blood, but not much. Thank God.

"Where were you hit?" Her voice sounded a lot shakier than she felt.

"You're okay?" Tarik's own voice was hoarse as he struggled to sit. "Can't hear a thing yet. Where's Eltsin?"

Jass noticed Tarik favoring his right arm. Oh Lord, he'd taken a bullet. Sympathetic pain squeezed at her heart. She helped him sit up and then tried to inspect his wound.

He batted her hands away. "It's fine. A scratch is all. Bullet only grazed me. What happened to Eltsin?"

She leaned in closer and spoke in his left ear. "He's dead. Sorry. I tried to aim for his gun arm, but he was moving too fast."

Tarik looked at her quizzically. "You took the time to aim? How good a shot are you?"

Beaming at him, she sat back on her heels. "Not bad."

She heard him groan as he tried to stand. "We need to stop the bleeding and get you to a doctor." Taking his left elbow, she assisted him to his feet.

Pulling his arm out of her grip, he scowled at her, spun around and went into the pantry, returning with a kitchen towel. "Can you find something to cut this into strips and fashion a bandage?"

She took the towel from his hand and, using her teeth, started a small tear in the end. "This do?" she asked while neatly ripping the material lengthwise with her two hands.

"A sharpshooter and a medic? Nice." He took a length of the makeshift bandage but shook his head after the first attempt. "A little help here?"

Sighing, she took back one end of the material and lent him a hand as he wound it around his upper arm.

"Looks like the bleeding's already stopped." Her breathing was finally evening out. "But it still might need suturing. And someone should definitely sterilize the surrounding area."

"Nonsense. I said it was fine. We have to get out of here before any of Eltsin's buddies come looking for their boss."

He was right about that. "Agreed. Any ideas how?"

"Can you drive? I could do it, but one-handed may become problematic if anyone's chasing us."

"Sure I can drive." She bit back a smart retort. "But where are we going to find a car?"

Tarik took her by the elbow this time and twisted her around, heading for the pantry again and the same way out as they'd come in. "Shakir left one of Eltsin's cars standing by for us. That way we'll also have easy access to the gate codes. Come on, your chariot awaits, Madame."

"What are you looking for?" Jass kept one hand on the steering wheel as she flipped on the overhead light.

They'd left Eltsin's house an hour ago and were now making the turns right below Corcovado mountain. With its huge arms outstretched over the city and its lights blazing brightly in the darkness of the forest surrounding the mountain, the 125-foot statue of Jesus at the top of Corcovado seemed to be offering its blessing to any who needed help. Jass would be happy to receive all the help she could get.

Tarik was rooting around in her backpack with his good arm. "Turn out the light," he demanded softly. "We'll be driving into the city lights soon enough. Besides, I can find your communicator by feel alone."

"Try the outside pocket." She turned off the interior lights and checked her rearview mirror for maybe the hundredth time since they'd left Eltsin's mansion. The road behind them was empty and dark.

"Are you hoping to reach Ed?" She had a few words for her handler herself.

"Or the local station chief."

"Hit the star button at the bottom. It's a direct line."

A few moments later, Tarik swore lightly under his breath. "No answer. Where is everyone?"

"Why don't you try reaching your brother?"

"I've been hesitating to contact Shakir. He might still be in a car along with the Taj. I don't want to break his cover."

"I think you'd better try him anyway. I don't like being out of touch when things have just gone to hell. We need advice and assistance."

Tarik clicked his comm and held his breath.

His brother's smooth, deep voice answered nearly right away. "Are you okay?"

"Fine. We're in the car you provided and headed down the mountain into Rio. Eltsin's dead. Where are the Taj agents?"

"They're about to board a flight to Miami. I'm putting on a disguise so I can board the plane with them. I've been afraid to get too close for fear they would recognize me as a Kadir. I had one of the local men drive them into Rio."

"Miami? Why there?" Tarik asked.

"I was hoping Eltsin could tell us that. Did you get any information out of the Russian before you killed him?"

Tarik wasn't about to tell his brother that he hadn't been the one to shoot their prime information source. "All I know is Eltsin said he'd sold the Taj some kind of new high-tech weapon-delivery system. He didn't give us a chance to ask anything else."

Shakir groaned. "Hell. I have to leave. I can't lose the Taj. And there's not another commercial flight to Miami for twelve hours. But I've arranged for you and Jass to take a U.S. military transport leaving Brazil right before noon. Bosque, the CIA station chief, will be waiting for you at your hotel room. He'll have instructions and passes."

Shakir didn't linger long enough to say anything else. He cut off and was gone.

Tarik relayed what his brother had told him. Jass didn't make a comment, but, through the dim dashboard lights, he watched her bite her lip.

"You're thinking the same thing I am?" He didn't like voicing his suspicions aloud, but had no choice. "That our traitor might be Bosque and we'll be walking into a trap at the hotel?"

"I've considered the possibility. But I want to gather my equipment from the hotel room. And how else are we going to get the passes we'll need for transport to Miami?"

Tarik sat quietly for a few moments, mulling over the possibilities. Finally he said, "We have no choice. But I have a plan."

"Oh, no. Not another plan. Lord help us."

As plans went, this one was somewhat better than the last brilliant idea Tarik had come up with. Jass straightened her borrowed maid's uniform and shoved the laundry cart in front of her down the hotel hallway.

"You need to go on a diet," she whispered, loudly enough for Tarik to hear. "This cart must weight a ton."

"Shussh," came the reply from deep under the dirty sheets and towels in the cart.

The hallways were silent at this hour. Six o'clock was too early for most hotel services and their luxury guests. But this was still a good disguise as far as Jass was concerned. As they drew closer to their room, she felt for her weapon under the cleaning supplies sitting on the cart's shelf.

After pulling the cart to a halt in front of their room, she immediately realized the door was ajar. "Trouble. The door's open."

Tarik stuck his head above the edge of the cart. "Wait," he whispered as he jumped out. "You go right. I'll take the left."

"What about your wounded arm?"

He frowned, then switched his weapon to his left hand and made her trade places. "On my mark."

Using the barrel of his gun, he pushed open the door as each of them waited with weapons at the ready on either side. But nothing happened.

Tarik held up his hand for her to keep her position and then he eased across the threshold. "I hear something."

Both of them slipped through the door and listened. Someone was groaning.

Jass clung to the wall as she carefully entered the main sitting room. There on the floor she saw Bosque, holding his bleeding head and moaning.

She stashed her weapon and went to him while Tarik checked the bathroom, bedroom and closet. "What happened, Bosque?"

"Ambush. I wasn't expecting it. Came out of nowhere." He groaned again.

Blood was everywhere. The place was in shambles. But Jass didn't smell any residual gun smoke. Obviously no one had fired bullets in this hotel room recently. Bosque's injuries had no doubt been inflicted with a heavy object and probably weren't life threatening. Tarik strode out of the bathroom carrying a towel, then held it to Bosque's forehead to sop up the blood.

"The place is clear," Tarik told them. "Whoever it was is gone. Call the desk and get a doctor up here."

She headed toward the desk phone, wondering what had been stolen from their room and who had taken it. She and Tarik hadn't left anything of real value in the room when they went to Eltsin's mansion. They'd taken all their high-tech toys and weapons with them. Except for her special CIA-issue laptop. Jass hadn't wanted to take the chance of Eltsin finding it. She'd locked it in the hotel safe as she'd packed.

After summoning a doctor and the hotel manager, Jass went straight to the safe. That door stood ajar exactly like the other one.

"They took my laptop," she called out.

When she came out of the closet, Tarik had Bosque sitting up in a chair. He was holding a wet towel to his forehead and the bleeding was down to a trickle.

Bosque gripped Tarik's arm. "Your papers and military passes are in my coat pocket. Take them and get out of here before anyone shows up and the questions start. I'll be okay."

Jass signaled for Tarik to grab the folder out of Bosque's coat. "Are you sure you didn't see anyone?"

Bosque moaned. "They came up from behind me."

"Have you heard anything from Ed Langdon,

Jass's handler?" Tarik had the papers in hand and seemed ready to charge out the door.

"Yes, I'm kind of worried about Ed." Jass didn't like not being able to reach the man she'd grown to care about over the years. "I haven't been able to reach him for hours."

"I haven't heard from him since yesterday morning." Bosque lifted his head. "But I'll take care of notifying him and the Task Force. Now beat it. All your instructions are in with your passes. Go."

Tarik grabbed her hand and dragged her toward the door. "Thanks, man. Take care of yourself."

Bosque weakly waved them away and went back to holding the towel to his forehead. Jass didn't like the idea of leaving him here. What if the bad guys came back?

"Tarik, are you sure we should…"

"Let's go. He'll be fine. He's armed. I felt

his undrawn weapon still in its holster when I pulled the passes from his coat."

"Still…"

"He's the CIA station chief. A big boy. And we can't miss our transport."

Tarik was right. But Jass's mind was whirling. Who had taken her laptop and left Bosque bleeding on the floor?

The ride on the air transport turned into one long and tedious affair for Tarik. Everything and everyone around him annoyed him beyond belief. Jass wouldn't let him rest until a medic cleaned and checked his wound. And when he'd tried to talk to her about who the traitor could be, she'd refused to discuss it, saying she needed time to think. Then instead of thinking, she'd passed out across two seats and slept for six hours straight.

Tarik knew what he thought. But he understood why she didn't want to consider—much less accept—the possibility. It seemed there could only be one person who had the means to accomplish everything that had happened. But if that were true, it would mean extremely bad news for Jass.

Still, they had to talk about it eventually.

Shakir met them at the airbase near Miami with a car. Jass had changed out of most of the Celile disguise on the plane, and she was back to looking like the woman he wanted to know a lot better. But she'd been too quiet. He knew the storm clouds in her heart were building to a terrible tempest. But if she wouldn't talk to him about it, how could he help her through it?

"Renting us motel rooms was tough at this time of year in Miami," his brother told them as he drove them off the airbase. "I wanted us all together so we can use our rooms as a temporary headquarters, but uh…well, here's the thing, you two have to share a room. Or, Tarik, you can bunk down on my floor. Your choice."

"No choice there. We're good sharing a room. We've been getting by that way. And we probably won't be here that long anyway." Tarik took a quick glance at Jass, who sat silently in the backseat. She said nothing. He guessed she had no complaints about the arrangements.

Shakir cleared his throat. "Okay, then. But we've lost the Taj, bugger it. Only temporarily, mind you. No need to sweat, they won't leave the area without us finding out. In the meantime, the men we left in Brazil finally managed to get a little information out of that henchman of Eltsin's we've been grilling." He actually smiled.

"Have you heard from the Task Force or from my handler?" Jass hadn't put together more than a few words since they'd left Brazil, and Tarik was happy to see her finally taking an interest again.

But he wished she'd asked anything else.

"Not a peep from your handler. But the Task

Force has been a big help here in the States."
Shakir drove the speed limit as the Miami sub-
urbs with their Spanish-style houses and their
ubiquitous palm trees rolled by the windows.
"They've paved the way for us and are assisting
in whatever ways we need them. And there're
more men available at your say-so. I think you
two have finally convinced them the Taj are, in
fact, international bad guys."

"What other intel did you get from Eltsin's
man?" Tarik needed to know where the biggest
danger lay.

"It appears that the nuclear delivery system
you heard about is state of the art. Small and
innocuous, it supposedly fits inside an ordinary
bottle or jar and will detonate with the usual
cell-phone call signal." Shakir exhaled sharply.
"But unlike the usual system, this device's explosion has a horrendous capacity because it's
assisted by a new kind of E-technology."

"Electro-magnetic pulse? How does that work?"

Shakir chuckled. "Beats me. But our resident genius, Karim, says this new technology is the stuff of nightmares—like Armageddon. A handheld device, remotely detonated, that can take out half a city the size of Miami? Chilling."

"But why Miami?"

"Yeah," Jass chimed in. "There don't seem to be any military or political targets here that are big enough or would cause enough of a show for high-profile terrorists like the Taj who're trying to make a splash."

"Good point." Shakir shot her a respectful glance in the rearview mirror. "We asked the man in Brazil that same question. He claims he doesn't know where they plan on using the device, but the Taj didn't receive their new toy while they were in Rio. They paid for it there and expect to pick it up here in Miami."

"Where?" Both Tarik and Jass asked the same question at the same time.

"It's supposedly coming in via ship container. According to Eltsin's man, the Taj agents plan on picking it up and personally taking it to its final destination. But the informant didn't know anything more concerning the actual pickup." Shakir furrowed his brow. "The biggest problem we face is there're two possible ports in the general Miami area where ship containers arrive daily."

"So that's it? That's all we know?" Frustration coursed through Tarik's whole body. How could they come this close and not finish the job?

"I might be of some help." Jass's quiet voice from the backseat brought a glimmer of hope.

Tarik turned as far as the seat belt would let him go. "What do you know?"

She halfheartedly shrugged one shoulder, but then spoke in a strong voice. "I tagged the elder of the two Taj agents while we were at dinner last night." She looked almost apologetic. "But we need the locating beacon software that goes with the GPS chip to find him. And that software was on the laptop that was stolen. If we can locate my handler or contact the local CIA office to borrow their software, we should be able to find that Taj agent by his chip."

"Consider it done," Shakir interjected. "I'm sure the Task Force will help. Good work."

Shakir dropped them and the car at the motel room and told them to get cleaned up and grab some much needed rest while he contacted the Task Force. Tarik didn't need sleep. What he needed was a long, serious discussion with Jass.

Their motel wasn't much. A two-story, cheap-looking affair with outside entry, it was near the Miami airport in a warehouse district. But when they went into their room, it was clean and neat with two double beds and a small but efficient kitchenette.

"Jass," he began when the outside door was locked behind them and they were by themselves.

"I don't want to talk about it." She grabbed the backpack and headed toward the bathroom. "I need a shower in the worst way first."

"Jass…"

"Alone, Tarik. This time I shower alone. Talk will come later." She slammed the door and disappeared.

She'd looked hurt. Without any words spoken between them, he knew her world was falling apart.

By the time she reappeared, he was already out of the cammos he'd changed into on the airplane courtesy of the U.S. Army and was ready to grab his own shower. He stood there like a fool with a blanket wrapped around his waist and watched her blow dry her hair in the big mirror over the tiny desk. She hadn't changed to her own clothes yet but wore only a towel to cover the parts of her body that he remembered well.

All that golden skin seemed pale and fragile in the low lighting of their room. In fact, Jass suddenly seemed fragile in a general way, though he knew that was nonsense. She'd taken out Eltsin without much remorse. She was a tough, professional covert agent of the United States government and nobody's fool.

But he knew she was hurting. And feeling all alone.

Hell. He was feeling pretty damned lonely himself.

He wanted to help her. He wanted for them to be closer. He wanted…

Without warning, he snapped. All the fear for her and the anger and the love—*Love? Yeah, love, damn it.* The realization of how he truly felt surged into his mind and drove desire along his nerve endings.

She stirred something in him that was

uncontrollable. Unstoppable. It was white hot and beyond explanation.

Never blinking while he ripped the dryer out of the wall plug and dragged her into his arms, she came willingly. He lasered his mouth over those delectable lips and kissed her long and hard.

When at last he came up for air, his breathing was ragged, and he was relieved to find her in the same condition. But one kiss wasn't enough. Not nearly enough to relieve the tension holding him hostage.

There could never be enough of her.

Chapter 15

Breathing hard, Jass knotted her hands in Tarik's hair. "I wish we had the time…."

His eyes were dark and so full of desire it left her breathless. "We may not get another time."

The unspoken understanding between them was real enough to be a solid thing. Not a barrier but more of a magnetic pull, drawing them closer when both of them knew it should not happen. Stupid or not, this was their time. Later may never come.

She saw the desire written clearly in his eyes

when he made the choice for both of them. Spewing out a curse to whatever gods threw obstacles into the paths of lovers, Tarik backed her up against the wall, pitched her towel in a corner and filled his hands with her aching breasts.

Pleasure, sharp and jolting, blossomed as he lowered his head and took one of her nipples into his mouth.

Pulling back to tease her with his tongue, Tarik murmured, "We still need to talk."

"Yeah." The tingles were already skipping along her spine and heading south. "I got that."

She frantically dragged his head lower and tried to keep him right where she needed him the most. "First this."

He nipped her gently and she keened his name. What he did made her forget everything. Made her crazy with lust. Made her stupid.

The next thing she knew he was already inside her, driving into her. She gripped his shoulders, dug her fingernails into his skin to urge him on. He helped her hook a leg around his hips, then grabbed her bottom with a firm hand, lifting and going deeper.

"Oh, yeah." She was out of breath and didn't care.

She didn't care about anything but letting him know the true depth of her feelings without using words. She took in all his fear for her along with his arousal. At the same time he seemed to lose all control and slammed them both off the map into oblivion.

Here was fire and passion. Here was a place she could belong. Here was her temporary refuge from cold, looming reality. Too soon, stars exploded behind her eyelids as they both reached that high, safe place as one entity.

A thousand heartbeats passed between them as they clung to each other, sharing air and a lifetime of wanting.

Slowly, he released her to slide to the floor.

"Steady?" he asked when she wobbled on her feet.

"I may never be steady again." She laughed, and when he laughed too, she knew her heart was lost to him for good.

Jass was delicious, all fresh from her shower yet sweat-dampened from making love. He felt drunk on her sweetness.

Still swimming in testosterone and half-crazed physical demands, Tarik managed one thought loud and clear. *This is love.* This is the way love is supposed to be.

He adored the way she'd called his name in the heat of passion. He adored her tiny gasps and the way she swallowed his desperate groans. He adored her quick mind and stark bravery. He plain adored her.

She started to turn away, but he swung her back and pressed his face to her neck. He would give her anything. Everything. His loyalty. His fortune. Anything he'd ever valued.

Moreover, he would even give her the scary things with no names—those reflections of the scared and lonely child he'd once been. The nightmares of being left alone that he'd kept hidden throughout the years. He would give her his life—and his whole future.

I love you, my little secret agent.

Jass held her hand to her pounding heart and chuckled deep in her chest. "As much as I hate to break this off, I have to dress. There's work to do." She backed up a step, stared up at him wide-eyed and smiling, and then headed to the bathroom.

Tarik took a deep breath and watched her walk away, knowing what had to come next.

As soon as she closed the bathroom door between them, he slipped into his clothes and called his brother on their family's satellite phone. "Where are you, Shakir?"

"We're about twenty miles north of the motel at one of the two shipyards. Our brother Darin has been working on the problem from his office. He had the idea that the container we're looking for would be shipped into a place where they could store containers." He cleared his throat. "And it seems only one of the two shipyards in the Miami area actually stores containers instead of shipping them back out directly. We're on our way there."

"Good thought. But I need your help on another matter. I have to find Ed Langdon, Jass's handler. I think he's the traitor and he's most definitely a missing link in the puzzle. We need to pick him up before he causes any more trouble."

"Why don't you have Jass contact him?"

"She tried while we were still in Brazil and no-go." And now she wouldn't even discuss the problem.

"Tell her to keep trying. Meanwhile, I'll

carefully inquire about him to the Task Force. Maybe they can help locate his current whereabouts."

Tarik thanked his brother and hung up just as Jass reappeared out of the bathroom. She looked so beautiful in her casual jeans and tank top that she took his mind away from the problems at hand.

Looking over at him, she absently put her hand to her hair and blinked. "What is it? Is my hair sticking straight up or something?"

He stood there shaking his head, over and over, without being able to utter a word. There was something still nagging at him. Something he'd forgotten while in his lust-filled haze. And it was something important.

The way he felt about her was simply astonishing. Never before in his entire lifetime had he needed anyone the way he needed Jass. All he wanted to do, all he could think about, was cocooning her in the warmth of his embrace and finding a way for the two of them to disappear off everyone's radar screens.

A silent beat came and went.

Oh, hell. That was it!

He schooled his voice and tone, trying not to frighten her. "Are you still tagged with a GPS chip?" he asked as casually as possible.

She shrugged. "Sure. I'm surprised you didn't…uh…feel it a little while ago. It's implanted under my left breast, right inside the crease."

"You need to remove that chip. Now." Okay, that was a little over the top. But he was fighting panic.

Jass laughed and ran her fingers through her hair. "You're nuts. The mission isn't over. I'll have it taken out when we're finished."

He swallowed hard and tried another tack. "Have you called your handler since we've landed in the States?"

She looked a slightly embarrassed. "Yeah.

Actually I've tried a couple of times with no luck. But I'm sure Ed will turn up pretty soon. At least, I hope Eltsin or the Taj didn't find him and hurt him. He should be okay, don't you think?"

"Jass…"

"No, don't say it. I don't want to talk about that." She wouldn't listen, but quickly turned and headed toward the motel-room door. "Have you heard from your brother? Let's go get something to eat unless you think Shakir needs us right away. I'm starving."

She threw open the door and bright sunshine spilled into the room, temporarily blinding him. When Tarik could focus again, he saw his worst nightmare standing at the threshold of the door.

"Ed!" Jass sounded pleased.

Obviously she didn't see the weapon in her handler's hand—or the younger of the Taj agents standing right beside him.

"Back in the room, Jass." Ed lifted the gun's barrel an inch and pointed it at Tarik. "Don't try anything, Kadir, or she'll be the first to go."

Jass took a step back, far enough that the two men could enter the room and close the door behind them. "What on earth is going on, Ed? Talk to me."

She still seemed oblivious to the weapon in Ed's hand. Tarik began to worry she was trying so hard to believe in her handler that she might get herself killed.

Reaching out, Tarik took her by the elbow, dragging her back to his side. "Ed's here for a reason. Let's hear him out."

"Sure," she said without looking at Tarik. She stood mutely, facing Ed and the weapon in his hand.

"Oh? He asks and now you listen? You wouldn't listen when I begged you to." Ed spit out the words with disgust. "I tried and tried to convince you to leave Kadir and abandon the mission. But you thought you knew better.

"Damn it, Jass," he went on, as a pained look appeared on his face. "Why'd you stop listening to me after all these years? Why with him?"

"I don't understand what you're saying." For the first time since Tarik had known Jass, her voice sounded weak.

"Yes, you do." Ed scowled. "You understand fine. You don't want to believe your own instincts. You've been playing that same game for years. Looking the other way when the things I did or said didn't add up. Time to grow up, Jass."

"Years? But…"

Tarik wanted to reach out to her. His every sense told him she needed him more than ever right now.

"Don't even think about it, Kadir." Ed pointed his gun directly at Jass's chest. "Give me one more chance to talk to her or watch her die before you."

Tarik would've loved to put his hands around Ed's neck and squeeze the traitorous life right out of him. But he knew Jass would have to hear the man out, as hard as it would be on her. He would give anything to protect the woman he loved from the coming pain, but this was one time when she had to be strong—alone.

The young Taj agent turned to Ed and spoke with a heavy accent. "Why are we waiting? You said you meant to kill them."

Ed waved the man off. "Give it a few more minutes first. There's time."

"Wait." Jass raised her chin and stared at Ed. "You're telling me you have always been— what? A traitor to your country? I don't believe it. You were my father's best friend. His partner. He died in your arms."

Ed chuckled. "Don't tell me you still believe the sappy story I made up? Jass, you have to be

smarter than that. I thought you were as intelligent as your old man."

Jass's body went ramrod straight. She fisted
her hands at her sides.

"Oh please," Ed said with a sigh. "You're
saying you didn't know your father was selling
secrets to the Russians? Or that he and I were
more than covert agent partners? And here all
this time I figured you were trying to learn the
ropes from me. That you and I would be the
same sort of business partners one day."

Jass took a tiny, nearly unnoticeable, step to
the left, covering Tarik's position with her own
body. He wanted to scream at her to stop it. To
get behind him and let him be the protector.
But he didn't dare call attention to what she
was doing or make any sudden moves.

But he did manage to secretly slide his arm
around behind his waist, fingering the weapon
in his belt. He was set. All he needed was a
small diversion.

"Tell me what really happened when my father died."

"Ah, come on, Jass. You don't want to hash this out right now. Just tell me you don't give a damn about Kadir and let's get out of here. There's a large fortune behind the deal. I'm willing to split it with you."

The Taj agent looked confused. Tarik imagined the man felt betrayed but couldn't be totally positive he understood because of the language difficulties.

"Okay, yes. But tell me about my father first."

The handler sighed. "You don't want to hear it. Not truthfully." Then the dirty double agent seemed to come to some private conclusion. "Oh, all right. Your father, my old partner Denny, suddenly decided he'd had enough. After years of our working deals together."

Ed waved his hand in the air. "Your old man said his change of heart had something to do with you. What a load of bull. But whatever it was that came over him, he wanted out. Pompous ass said he would go to our CIA superiors and rat on our Russian contacts." He shrugged carelessly. "Well, I couldn't let him do that, could I?"

Jass drew a breath and whispered, "So you killed him."

Ed caught her words and scowled. "Of course, I killed him. The bastard was going to turn me in."

Something in Ed's manner changed. He tensed as though ready to fire. Tarik palmed his weapon and balanced his stance in preparation.

"I'm sorry to do this, Jass. Really. But you've left me no choice."

"Ed...no..."

Instead of firing at Jass or trying to get Tarik first, Ed swung his body to the left and shot the stunned Taj agent directly through the forehead at point-blank range.

"This is the best plan," Ed murmured as the body went down. "A big shoot-out will work to my benefit. All of you will have died trying to kill the others."

Tarik could see the handler's arm muscles tightening again and realized what came next.

"Duck!" All Tarik could do was react—and pray.

Jass went down like a stone while he pumped three silenced rounds into the surprised double agent, who had turned to fire at Jass but never got off the first shot.

With no loud gun blasts, the sickening sounds of bullets hitting flesh competed for attention with the sight of blood spatter as Ed crumpled to the floor. Tarik waited for any further movement, but none came.

"Tarik!" The smoke hadn't even cleared when Jass jumped up and spun around. "Oh my god, are you hit?"

Tarik opened his arms and she fell into them, clinging to him as tears sprouted on her cheeks.

"I'm not hit and it's all over, love," he murmured soothingly. "I'm fine. And you're going to be okay."

He knew her real wounds were hidden and went deep. That it might take years for her to get over what she'd had to face. Her whole life had been a sham. How was anyone supposed to put that aside and go on?

But he would be there for her—however long it took.

Letting her sob into his shoulder, Tarik threw a glance at the handler and the Taj agent laying still in growing pools of blood. They were both gone for good.

It didn't take too long for Jass's tears to subside, but she didn't move out of his embrace. Tarik figured she would be going into shock at any moment and needed professional attention.

"Let me call Shakir," he whispered. "Get him

over here to deal with the bodies so I can take you to the hospital."

"I don't need a hospital. I wasn't hit. But I need to finish this mission." She reared back and threw a quick look over her shoulder at the two dead men on the floor. "How're we going to find that delivery device now?"

Tarik sighed and let loose of his hold on the too-tough covert agent. "You need to stop now, Jass. Let me and my family handle things from here. Go home. I'll find you and let you know how things turn out. I want you to take enough time to get your head together."

Jass frowned and stepped away. "My head is okay." She folded her arms protectively around her middle. "Maybe this revelation was a bit of a shock, but not completely out of the blue. Despite what you and Ed must've thought of me, I'm not totally stupid. I wouldn't discuss it because I wanted to talk things over with Ed first.

"The sight of his weapon changed everything," she admitted. "I decided to play along for info."

Tarik didn't know what to say to her, or what to do *for* her. She needed help, but while she was in covert-agent mode, he would never get her to accept it.

When he didn't say anything for a long time, she said, "I was serious. Time is short. A maid could stumble in here at any moment. Do you have any thoughts on how to find the delivery system now?"

"There's still that chip you planted on the elder Taj agent. Shakir is working on getting the CIA software that we need."

Jass stepped out of his immediate space, leaving him feeling more alone than ever.

"Ed may have killed the other Taj agent, too." She pointed down at the dead body closest to her feet. "Judging by the expression on this young Taj's face, it wouldn't surprise me if the kid thought he and Ed were a team, double-crossing his boss. But he trusted the wrong man, poor kid. Triple crosses didn't seem to be out of the question for good old Ed."

Tarik looked down at the Taj agent, too and noticed something he hadn't seen before. Bending on one knee, he pushed the kid's loose long-sleeved shirt up past his elbow, allowing him to study what appeared to be a new tattoo on the boy's forearm.

"What are you looking at?" Jass bent to study the image, too. "The tattoo? What about it?"

The picture was of a dagger. Not an unusual decoration for the Taj Zabbar—when it came to pictures or images. But body decorating was not something the Taj accepted.

"It's new." Tarik touched the outline. "Done within the last twelve hours."

"You mean this kid must've stopped here in Miami long enough to get a tattoo? That is odd." She peered closer, studying the decoration. "Do you see this? Look, along the knife blade. Is that some kind of writing or hieroglyphics?"

Tarik bent his head lower. "They're numbers, written in the Taj Zabbar language."

"What does it mean?"

He sat back on his heels and thought about why a young Taj agent would take the time to do something like getting a tattoo when that was so abhorrent to his culture. There was only one reason Tarik could think of—money.

"What if this set of numbers corresponds to the marking on the container holding the delivery device?" he muttered almost to himself.

"Now that's a clever thought." Jass straightened up and folded her arms over her chest. "Shipping containers all look alike with the only difference being their number designation. I like it. Can we find someone to translate those numbers into something we can understand?"

"No problem." Tarik stood, went to the desk and retrieved paper and a pen.

"Oh? Who do you have in mind?"

He came back and starting copying down the numbers. "You're looking at him."

Adrenaline overload let-down. Jass was familiar with the symptoms, but the shock-like feeling was still a pain in the butt. She brushed past the shakes as they threatened to send her to the floor and produce serious quantities of tears. Going through the motions on autopilot, she grabbed her backpack and left the room with Tarik on their way to the port and one of the shipping container storage areas.

After the motel-room door closed behind them and the sight of all that blood and gore disappeared, she gulped down another breath and fought the onslaught of nausea. *Damn it.* She refused to be this weak.

Just because a few moments ago she'd learned

that her father had been a double agent—and her beloved friend Ed had killed him—was no reason to collapse when there was still a job to be done. Jass prided herself on being calm in the midst of chaos. No allowances for personal dramas.

She took a stab at being flip. "I'm sure glad your shooting arm was tended by that medic on the plane. You can thank me later for nagging you about it. Good shot, by the way."

"Good ducking," Tarik answered as he opened the car door and let the buildup of hot air escape before climbing in to turn on the A/C.

Their partnership was almost at an end. He would soon go off to fight more of his family's battles. And she would be stuck in endless rounds of post-shooting debriefs.

Just as well. She wasn't sure she could handle dealing with her newfound feelings for Tarik at the same time as she was dealing with life-changing knowledge about the people whom she'd thought loved her.

Greed. It had all been about greed. Her own father had sold out his country for money.

Heartbreak and pain. Too much of both were threatening to consume her. She wasn't ready to face either one.

For now she shoveled all her baggage, questions and misery into a corner of her mind to deal with another time.

Tarik set the GPS and drove the car out of the motel's parking lot.

"Do we know where we're going?"

He shot her a quelling glance and pulled his SAT phone out of his pocket. "I'm calling Shakir to send someone to take care of everything here. And to give him a head's up on this container number. Maybe he can narrow down the possibilities."

"Good idea. There's probably hundreds of containers in the storage yard."

It turned out there were more like thousands of containers in ten different yards. Every minute of the day containers were being off loaded from ships and sent to storage. Then those containers were eventually loaded onto semi-tractor-trailers for shipment by truck throughout the U.S.

Shakir met them at one of the yards. "We're most fortunate to have a genius in our family."

"Cousin Karim? What'd he find out?"

"He was able to hack into the shipyard computers and track the container by its number. It should be somewhere in this yard."

Jass scanned a glance over the many containers. Then she noticed a nearly quarter-mile-long line of trucks waiting to be checked out of the yard with their shipping containers now securely attached to their tractors like any other load.

She turned to Tarik and Shakir. "Are we sure

that container hasn't already been loaded onto one of those trucks?"

Tarik looked over her head at the line of semis. "You take left. I'll take right."

"I'll stop the trucks at the gate," his brother called out as all of them scattered in different directions.

Jass pulled her weapon from her backpack and took off down the line, checking numbers as she ran. About ten containers later, she was huffing and stopped to take a breath.

When she looked up into the cab of the next truck, she spotted a driver with his ball cap pulled low on his forehead. But Jass couldn't miss those black, beady eyes. The elder Taj agent!

He looked up then too and their eyes met, held. Then he disappeared. Jass dashed around the front of the truck and found him climbing down out of the cab.

"Hold it." She held her weapon with both

hands, training it on his substantial gut. "It's over."

Instead of raising his arms in surrender, the elder Taj turned and ran.

Jass roared, all the frustration and anger rising to the surface, and leaped on his back, slamming him to the hot asphalt. Air escaped his lungs as she rammed her knee into his back and pressed the barrel of her gun to the back of his neck.

"Don't give me a reason to pull the trigger." Shaking badly by the time he groaned out his acceptance, she tried to release her finger, but her hand was frozen on the gun.

"You're done, my love." Tarik appeared, standing over her and easing the weapon from her hand. "Let go, Jass. The mission is finished. Let me take over from here."

Her hand opened for him, only for him, and sudden uncontrollable tears blinded her to everything else.

Chapter 16

"I want to see her." Tarik scowled at his brother. "I don't understand why the powers-that-be insisted on separating us." It had been nearly six hours since they'd captured the Taj elder and recovered the nuclear delivery device, and he hadn't caught sight of Jass in the last five.

Nearly sunset by now, tourists on the beaches would be ordering cocktails or having beers with their friends. But the Kadirs, the Task Force and the local CIA were more or less imprisoned at the Broward County Sheriff's office, waiting for General Wainwright to arrive and take charge of the situation.

The CIA had spent the whole day taking Jass's statement in one of the interrogation rooms. Tarik hadn't liked it. Hadn't liked the chalky look of her skin or the sunken appearance of her eyes when they'd ridden in the back of the sheriff's cruiser over here. He'd wanted her to see a doctor. Maybe even a whole staff of psychologists.

Instead, Jass had agreed to be sequestered to tell her old superiors at the CIA what little she knew of her handler's secret activities. Without Ed alive to grill, the CIA and the Department of Defense would have to piece together the real story of treason from old files and Jass's memories.

"I understand they're moving her to D.C. in a little while." Shakir stood quietly with his hands folded behind his back. "Our job's done here, brother. We located the delivery device and now the DOD, the State Department and the entire Executive Branch will have to accept that the Taj Zabbar are dealing in international terror."

"They should've listened a year ago when we tried to warn them." Tarik's patience was wearing thin, but he didn't want to tick off his own brother. "Do we know whether the Taj elder has told them anything yet?"

"Are you serious? Someone from the Pentagon showed up this morning at the container yard near Port Everglades and whisked that elder Taj agent away as an enemy combatant. He's long gone.

"But our brother Darin's people have retrieved interesting tidbits from the internet," Shakir continued with a smug smile. "According to the Net, the Taj agents were supposed to drive that truck with the delivery system all the way to Washington D.C. They'd plotted to detonate the nuclear device either beside the Capitol or the Pentagon. Planned on making a big splash. And force the U.S. imperialist machine to sit up and take notice."

Tarik was amazed. "After all this secrecy, the Taj themselves planned to publicize their terrorist dealings to the world?"

"In a big way."

Tarik began to pace the tiny conference room where they'd been waiting for hours. "Do we know how they managed to get Ed Langdon in on the deal?"

"Big payoffs, would be my bet. That Russian in Brazil, Eltsin, used to be connected to the Russian mafia. He'd probably worked with Langdon years ago when he was a double agent."

"Langdon was a real piece of work. He planned on killing his partners along with Jass and then telling the Task Force they'd killed each other."

"Scumbag," his brother retorted.

"I want to see Jass," Tarik said between gritted teeth. "Before she leaves. What do I have to do to convince—?"

"Sorry, Kadir." General Wainwright appeared at the door. "She's flying to D.C. within the hour. The Task Force will be going through a major overhaul over the next few months. The idea that two of our own were double agents and one of them endangered an entire mission has shaken everyone."

The general came all the way into the room and closed the door behind him. "I don't suppose I could talk you into coming back as a consultant to help us sort through the intel?"

"No, sir. I'm sure my family still needs me. I doubt the Taj Zabbar are going to be any happier with the Kadir family now that their grandiose terror plot has been ruined."

The general nodded. "Only *temporarily* ruined, would be my guess. I understand. But if you can find a way to consult for both of us, the Kadirs and the U.S. government, the offer remains open."

"I appreciate that, sir."

"In the meantime," the general went on. "The President has asked to see you and your brother. I think he wants to thank you for being on our side."

"Yes, sir. Now?" Tarik asked.

"Tomorrow morning. We'll be taking a military flight back to Andrews at 8 a.m. However, I'm sorry you won't be able to enjoy any of the south Florida activities this evening, gentlemen. The President has granted you diplomatic immunity, but there's still a lot of questions we will be answering for the sheriff and Homeland Security tonight."

Tarik wasn't going to leave it at that. "Yes, sir. But…I need to see Jass before she leaves. Can you arrange it?"

"She hasn't been asking to see you, son. I'm sorry…"

"A couple of moments is all I need. It's a matter of life and death."

It was. His life. He would die if he didn't get a chance to talk to her before she disappeared into her world of secret agents.

The general actually smiled. "All right. It wouldn't be my fault if we just happened to be leaving the office to grab a bite of dinner at the same time as they were leaving for the airport, would it?" He checked his watch. "I'll speak to the sheriff about sending a deputy with us for security. Be in the parking lot in ten minutes."

Tarik nearly saluted the general as he smartly spun around and left.

Rubbing suddenly sweaty palms against his thighs, Tarik turned to his big brother. "What can I say to her in only a few minutes in a public parking lot?"

Shakir shrugged. "Say what you feel. I've found that's the only thing that works well with the woman you love."

Jass would give up a day of her life for a shower. In fact, she would gladly give up *this* day. It had so far been the absolute worst.

Except, of course, for the few minutes she'd spent alone with Tarik this morning in their motel room. That was something she would never give away. The memories were going to have to hold her for the rest of her life.

"Wait here," her CIA companion and guard told her as they entered the late-afternoon heat of the open parking lot. "I'll bring the SUV around."

As the young man sprinted off, she stood, tapping her toe against the searing asphalt and thinking about Tarik. She hadn't said goodbye. But then that was probably for the best.

What they'd done—what they'd been to each

other on this mission—it was special. But it was over. She couldn't afford to look back.

Closing her eyes, she let the dull ache of never seeing him again wash over her. More pain.

She had enough pain on her plate already. That's why years ago, when her father went away and left her with a mother who'd never loved anyone but herself, Jass had erected those walls around her emotions. To keep the pain and loneliness at bay. Tarik had climbed those walls and she wished to hell that she'd kept him out. Letting Tarik stay in her world for any longer now would only open her up to more heartbreak than she thought she could withstand.

"Jass! Wait up."

Turning to the familiar voice, she bit down on her lip to keep from crying out his name. Oh Lord, the man was sinfully gorgeous.

A single tear threatened to leak from the corner of her eye but she willed it back. "I'm…

leaving, Tarik. There's no time to—" She bit her tongue. "Well, to say goodbye."

He put his hands on her upper arms, holding her firmly but gently. "Are you okay?" He looked at her as though she were the most precious jewel in a crown full of expensive diamonds.

"I will be." She stood straighter and eased out of his grip. "General Wainwright has arranged for me to spend a little time in psych eval at Walter Reed, starting tonight. It'll be like a nice short vacation before the real work of reorganizing the Task Force begins."

"Good. That's good. They'll help you." Tarik reached out a hand. But when she stepped away, he dropped it back to his side.

"Jass, I want to see you again. There're things we..." He looked around at the busy parking lot. "We need to talk. I'm flying to D.C. in the morning to see the President. But if you'll be in the hospital for a few days, I'll wait."

She began shaking her head. Unable to say what needed to be said. Unable to cut him out of her life forever when that was exactly her best course of action.

"Don't do this." His voice tensed, strained. "You know we're not done, damn it. Not by a long shot."

A big, black SUV pulled up alongside her, the driver leaving its motor rumbling in neutral. Relieved to have an escape route, she opened the passenger door.

"This is for the best, Tarik. We come from different places. There's nothing I can add to your life. Forget me. Forget us. Go save your family and the world."

Tears were threatening to spill over. But she refused. She turned her back on the only man left on earth who mattered to her at all and climbed into the SUV.

"Jass..." Tarik stood there with his hands

fisted at his sides and the saddest expression on his face.

She would never forget the way he was looking at her. Not in a million years.

"Goodbye, Tarik. Take good care of yourself."

Slamming the door, Jass held tightly to the handle because otherwise she might fly off into oblivion. She held on and kept swallowing hard as the SUV pulled out of the lot.

Running away. Yes, it was true. She was scared and running as fast as she could from a relationship that was bound to cause her more pain than her battered heart would ever be able to withstand.

Four weeks. Tarik's need to see Jass, to be with her, grew ever more insistent as the days dragged on.

He stood, staring out the window of his hotel room suite at the sun setting over the Potomac.

Cherry blossoms blew in the spring breezes, and at times the city looked so romantic it made his heart ache with loneliness.

But he wasn't alone. Various members of his family had arrived in D.C. over the weeks, hoping to convince him to give up his quest and come back with them.

No chance.

This was crazy. How could the one person he'd fallen for hard be the one person who refused to even talk to him?

It must be some kind of perverted justice. Retribution for a life spent playing games and hiding behind hundreds of different faces.

But Tarik rejected what everyone else thought was his fate. Jass had sent him a message the other day explaining that they had nothing left to say to each other. He didn't agree. He had a lot left to say. And wanted a lifetime to say it.

"Are you sure you don't want to go out to dinner with us, Tarik?" Rylie, one of his new sisters-in-laws, appeared in the doorway of the suite's second bedroom.

She and Darin were here in Washington ostensibly to take a second honeymoon. Tarik knew the real reason why they'd come. The same reason the rest of his family had shown up at various times over the last month.

"No. But, thanks."

"You can't sit around forever and mourn a relationship that didn't get off the ground." Rylie came closer and spoke softly. "I know it's hard for you. You've never been turned down before. But sometimes no just means no. That's when you need to accept things the way they are and go on with your life."

He exhaled sharply but said nothing.

"Come back to the Mediterranean with us." She laid a gentle hand on his arm. "Your family still needs you, bubba. We love you and want you with us."

Swallowing down the threatening tears, Tarik

forced a smile at his sister-in-law and her Texas twang. "Yeah, the Task Force says they need me, too. But I can't work. I can't do anything yet. I have to talk to her, Rylie. There has to be a way."

But neither the Task Force nor the CIA would give him Jass's phone number or address. He'd sent message after message. Knowing full well nothing would work as well as it would if he could take her in his arms and tell her in person.

"There could be a way." Darin came out of the bedroom already dressed in his expensive designer suit. "Ambush might be a little extreme, but I trust she wouldn't call the cops on you if you simply showed up at her apartment."

Rylie didn't look happy with her husband, but she stepped back and folded her arms over her chest, staying silent for the moment.

"I can't locate her address or, believe me, I would try."

Darin waved his arm in the air as he shot his cuffs. "Nonsense. Call Karim. If anyone can find her, he can."

"Darin!" Rylie scowled at her husband. "Don't tell your brother to do something like that. The CIA would be furious with Tarik if he had Karim hack into their system. Not to mention how unhappy Jasmine O'Reilly will be if he simply shows up at her place."

Darin shrugged. "It's his life, sweetheart. Let him try."

Tired and cranky, Jass climbed into her sweats and opened all the windows in her apartment to let the brisk nighttime breeze cool off her overheated brow. Another day from hell was finally behind her.

All she wanted was to do now was turn the TV on to some thoughtless channel and vegetate on the couch while she contemplated her future. She refused to spend any more time with the psychologists. Enough was enough.

The one she'd seen today actually had the nerve to tell her she would have to go through all the stages of grief in order to heal. The same as if a loved one had died. The fool doctor said learning about Ed had been a kind of death of innocence and she needed to grieve.

Bull. What she needed was a lot less new-age crap.

The fact was, she'd turned in her resignation from the Task Force to General Wainwright last week and was now free to do as she pleased. And what would please her was to be left alone to think.

The general had said, "But we need you on our side."

Not anymore they didn't. Every man in the Task Force knew the story of Ed's traitorous dealings. How could she live with that on the job? How could she explain that she'd never known?

The CIA had pieced together enough facts to learn that her father was not the traitor Ed had claimed he'd been. The news was a relief of sorts. But in Jass's mind the new information simply made her father seem incredibly dense for not recognizing what his partner had been up to.

Of course, she hadn't seen Ed for what he really was over the last ten years either. And that was something she would have to someday settle in her own mind. But talking to a bunch of shrinks had not been helping.

The only one of them who'd made a lick of sense had said she should consider this an opportunity to begin again. To start a brand new life.

How right he was. She'd already quit her job—she had enough in savings that she didn't need to go to work again anytime soon. She would take the time to rethink her life. Maybe she would even go back and get her law degree the way her dad always wanted.

One thing was for sure—she would be moving out of this apartment. As of tomorrow. It reminded her too much of the past. Jass even wanted to move out of D.C., but she wasn't sure where to go.

And yes, she knew that meant she was running away again. So what? No amount of distance would erase the real problem—her memories of Tarik. He was always there, in her mind, talking to her. Consoling her. Being her friend when everyone else around her only wanted something or saw her as a job.

Changing what she did for a living and where she slept at night was not going to change how she felt about Tarik one iota. And she'd finally come to the conclusion she didn't want it to change. Thoughts and dreams of Tarik would keep her company throughout the years.

She'd given up on the idea of ever trying love again with anyone else. Where would she find someone with the same blinding smile? Or with Tarik's way of being in tune with her thoughts? Or with those same soft, mushy gazes whenever he looked in her direction?

She hadn't received a message from him in the last couple of days. Good for him. She hoped he'd given up and left the area. He deserved a new start, too.

She couldn't live with herself if she'd caused him any real hurt. Surely these messages she'd been receiving from him all stemmed from a wounded pride. He'd overcome that soon enough.

He was a special person. She didn't think she'd ever met anyone as strong and determined as Tarik Kadir.

Or as warm and loving. Or as sexy and erotic.

Giving herself permission to have yet another crying jag, she rolled over on the couch and buried her face in the pillow. *Have a good life, my love.*

* * *

God, he must be seriously in love to take his life in his hands this way.

Tarik was so nervous that his whole body shook as he lowered himself to the apartment ledge under an endless star-filled sky. But it wasn't the idea of dangling in midair again that made him shaky. It was knowing he would only get one chance with Jass.

When his feet finally hit solid surface, he balanced precariously on the narrow ledge and unbuckled his harness. He was more wired from nerves than from the flying device. Which only went to show how important Jass was to him.

He'd been afraid to try knocking on her door. Too easy for her to lock him out and send him away. And then he'd caught a break and discovered her windows were open.

No fire escape and no balcony. But hell, he couldn't let that stop him.

Inching along the ledge, Tarik held his breath

and refused to consider the dark abyss below. He tried to think of all the things he wanted to say, but his mind went blank as he set one foot inside her window.

"Hold it." Jass's voice was loud and strong through the darkness. "Come on inside but watch your step. This .38 has a hair trigger."

Yeah, he would bet it did. "It's me, Jass. Put your weapon down."

She stepped aside and flicked on a table lamp but held the gun on him as he climbed inside. "What on earth do you think you're doing, Kadir?"

Dressed in winter running sweats and heavy socks, she wasn't wearing a speck of makeup. That amazing head full of chestnut hair was standing straight up in spikes. And those exotic hazel eyes had darkened to the deepest green and were wary as hell.

Yes indeed, her protective walls were still

high and tight. He'd have a devil of a war coming in order to break them down.

"How are you doing, Jass?"

"Fine. Why are you here? You should've gone back to your family by now." She was still holding the gun, but the barrel had dipped to point at his feet and she'd released her finger from the trigger.

"I need a little of your time."

"And that means you come in through my window in the middle of the night? You're lucky I didn't shoot you in the ass and ask questions later."

"Hey, and thanks for that. Grand gesture on your part considering not many bad guys could fly into your window five stories up."

The corners of her lips tipped up at that remark and she dropped her weapon to her side. "All right. Come in and sit down. Tell me whatever it is and then go away."

He didn't want to leave this woman. Not ever

again. *Man up, bubba,* as Rylie would say. Time to face love down.

"Look." He sunk into a side chair and hoped she would sit on the couch beside him. "There's something I didn't say the last time we were together. That was a mistake. I…"

"The only thing I want to hear from you is that you're leaving and starting a new life. Do what's best for everyone, Tarik." She averted her gaze, refusing to meet his eyes.

He'd expected a war. Still, her words hit him like a nuclear warhead.

Standing again, he tried to keep the whine out of his voice. "You don't even want to hear me out? I thought…we cared about each other. Is that how you treat people you care about?"

She shot him a quick glance, then stared at the floor. But in that instant he'd seen longing. Regret. Hope.

He was at her side in a click. He put her gun on the table but then stayed his hands, kept them from drawing her close. "I know you're afraid. But…"

"I'm not afraid of anything."

Oh, his sweet love. "Right. I get it. You're not afraid of anything but me. And of the possibilities of love."

"There is no such thing as love." She backed up and sat on the couch with her hands clutched in her lap.

"Not true, Jass. I know because I'm in love with you."

He heard her soft whimper and it threw him back to a time when she'd closed her eyes and climaxed around him. A vivid image of the two of them soaring was not what he needed to stay strong right now.

"You don't know what you're saying," she finally managed in a tight voice. "It was just the job. We had to be lovers and…uh…things got carried away. You'll get over it."

Tarik thought he'd better sit before he fell

over. She was a tough one to crack. She'd been hurt too much in her life. He plopped down beside her and took her in his arms.

She began to protest, but he folded her into his chest. "Shussh, my love. I'm not going to get over loving you anytime soon. I figure it might take a thousand years or so. Is that enough time to convince you?"

"Don't talk crazy." Her words were almost interrupted by a sob, but she held on. "It was a job. We were partners."

"Oh? So you've slept with your partners on other jobs?"

"Of course not." She reared back with tears in her eyes.

"Then I meant something to you." He held her tight and let his gaze tell her how he felt. "We belong together, Jass. People who love each other should be together."

"Oh, you should see your face," she said in a

rough voice. "At the love clearly shining in your eyes. No one has ever looked at me that way before."

Finally able to breathe again, he relaxed his shoulders as she pressed kisses over his eyelids and along his forehead, signaling the war was over. Soon, though, he couldn't stand sitting still and relaxation flew out the open window. He plundered her mouth slowly. Deeply.

"This is a first for me," she told him through breathless tears. "No one has ever loved me the way you do."

"Stick with me, sweetheart. Our life is going to be filled with lots of love and lots of firsts."

"I love you, too, Tarik." She smiled up at him and sniffed back more tears.

"Good thing. It's always good to love the man you're going to marry."

She laughed as he kissed her again. This time without the urgency. But with the intensity of a man making a lifetime promise. A lifetime he suddenly knew would definitely be worth all the trouble.

Epilogue

"Come walk on the beach with me."

Jasmine O'Reilly Kadir looked up from the table to find her husband of one week standing over her with his hand outstretched. Moonlight shined on his face as the soft sounds of the tempting Mediterranean washing ashore sent romantic music to her ears. That same mischievous look was back in Tarik's eyes. She'd always known that look would cause her big trouble.

"Not fair, Tarik." Shakir's wife, Nikki, who

was sitting next to her at the table, gave her brother-in-law a pout. "You didn't give us a chance to meet your bride before you two married. And not even giving us enough time to come to your wedding was just plain wrong. We're only now getting to know her. Sit down and have a drink with us."

Shakir stood up from the table. "Time for that later, Nik. Let the lovebirds have their honeymoon in peace. For now, come walk on the beach with me."

Nikki looked flustered, but she rose beside her husband. "Will the kids be okay for…?"

"The kids are fine. Come on." The two of them wandered off down the beach.

Still seated at the table, Rylie laughed and sipped her drink. "Well, I want to hear what y'all have planned for your future, Tarik. Are you staying here with us and working for the Kadirs? Or will you be going back to the U.S. and working for the Task Force?"

Jass answered first as she reached up and took her husband's hand. "Both. The Task Force needs Tarik's expertise to put them back on the right track. And I've told Darin I would be happy to help train covert agents for the Kadirs since it looks like the Taj Zabbar aren't about to give up their vendetta against the family any-time soon."

"Yes, and we're grateful, sister." Darin walked up to the table from out of the darkness and stood behind his wife. "Especially cousin Karim. He wants to be your first pupil."

Darin glanced down at Rylie and put his hand on her shoulder. "Come walk on the beach with me, wife. There's a beautiful moon."

He didn't have to ask Rylie twice.

Tarik gently pulled Jass to her feet as Darin and Rylie went off in the other direction. A wicked thrill rushed through her. She could scarcely believe how lucky she was. That this wonderful man loved her was still a shock. But a good shock.

"I'm not that crazy about the sand," she said as she laid her hands against his chest and looked up into his eyes.

"Thank God." Tarik slid his arm around her shoulders and turned them around to head in the direction of their apartment. "Let's go home."

Sighing, Jass let her husband's love wash over her like the music of the sea. They had all the time in the world to walk on beaches and talk about their pasts. The rest of their lives. She would never tire of being with him.

As Tarik said, "I may stop loving you some day—oh, in about a thousand years or so."

* * * * *

Discover Pure Reading Pleasure with

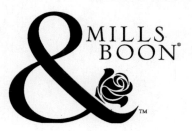

Visit the Mills & Boon website for all the latest in romance

Buy all the latest releases, backlist and eBooks

Find out more about our authors and their books

Join our community and chat to authors and other readers

Free online reads from your favourite authors

Win with our fantastic online competitions

Sign up for our free monthly eNewsletter

Tell us what you think by signing up to our reader panel

Rate and review books with our star system

www.millsandboon.co.uk

 Follow us at twitter.com/millsandboonuk

 Become a fan at facebook.com/romancehq